Nicole  'Dell
TRUTH OR DARE
Interactive Fiction for Girls

Published by Barbour Publishing, Inc., P.O. Box 719, Uhrichsville, Ohio 44683, www.barbourbooks.com

Our mission is to publish and distribute inspirational products offering exceptional value and biblical encouragement to the masses.

ec̸pa Member of the
Evangelical Christian
Publishers Association

Printed in the United States of America.

Nicole 'Dell
TRUTH OR DARE
Interactive Fiction for Girls

BARBOUR
PUBLISHING

*This book is dedicated to my mom, Carolyn,
who cried when she read it. I never understood, until
I became a mother myself, how much heartache could
come from watching a child face important, life-altering
decisions. Mom, your long-suffering faith in God and
unconditional love for me inspire me as a mother
and a writer to make the decision-making process
easier for young girls. I love you, Mom.*

Chapter 1

RULE THE SCHOOL

The first bright yellow light of day was starting to peek through the blinds covering her window. Lindsay Martin stretched and yawned as she slowly woke up. After tossing and turning much of the night, she was still sleepy, so she turned over and pulled the puffy pink comforter up to her chin and allowed herself to doze off for a few more minutes, burying her face in the coolest spot on her pillow.

But wait! Suddenly, Lindsey sat up quickly and threw back the covers, remembering that it was the first day of school. And, with no time to waste, she jumped out of bed.

She had carefully selected her clothes the night before; the khaki pants and screen-print tee were still hanging on her closet door, just waiting to be worn. But after thinking about it, they seemed all wrong. Frantically plowing through her closet for something different to wear, Lindsay pushed aside last year's jeans and T-shirts and found the perfect outfit: not too dressy, not too casual, not too anything. As an eighth grader, she wanted to look cool without looking like she was trying too hard—which was the fashion kiss of death. Confident that she had selected the perfect outfit, she padded off to the bathroom to get ready to face the day.

Happy with how she looked—jeans with just the right amount of fading down the front, a short-sleeved T-shirt layered over a snug long-sleeved T-shirt, and a pair of sunglasses perched atop her blond hair—she bounced down the stairs, slowing as she reached the bottom. Just wanting to get out of the house and be on her way, Lindsay sighed when she recognized the smell of bacon coming from the kitchen. "Mom, I'm really not hungry, and I have to go meet the girls!"

"Now you know I'm not going to let you head off to school without breakfast, so at least take this with you." Mom held out Lindsay's favorite breakfast sandwich: an English muffin with fluffy scrambled eggs, cheese, and two slices of bacon.

Lindsay wrapped it up in a napkin so she could take it with her and gave her mom a quick kiss before rushing out the door. "Thanks, Mom. You're the best!"

Hurrying toward the school, Lindsay munched on her sandwich along the way. Nerves set in, and halfway through her sandwich, her stomach rebelled; she tossed what was left into a nearby trash can, where it fell with a thud.

After her short walk down the tree-lined streets, she arrived at the meeting spot—a large oak tree in the front yard of the school—about fifteen minutes early. Shielding her eyes from the sun and squinting in eager anticipation, Lindsay watched the street for the first sign of her three best friends. She expected Sam and Macy to arrive by school bus—they lived too far away from the school to walk, so they generally rode the bus together. Kelly lived close enough to walk, but her mom usually dropped her off before heading to her job as an attorney in the city. Lindsay was thankful that she lived so close to the school. She loved being the first one there to greet her friends each morning. Since her mom didn't have to leave for work and Lindsay didn't need to catch the bus, she had a bit more flexibility and could save a spot for them under their favorite tree.

The bus pulled into the driveway, squealing as it slowed. It paused to wait for the crowd of students to move through the crosswalk. When it finally parked, the doors squeaked open and students began to pour off the bus just as Kelly's mom pulled up to the curb right in front of Lindsay.

"Bye, Mom!" Kelly grabbed her new backpack out of the backseat and jumped out of the car. At almost the same time, Macy and Sam exited the bus after the sixth and seventh graders got off.

Excitedly the four girls squealed and hugged each other under their tree, never minding the fact that they had been with each other every day for the entire summer. They shrieked and jumped up and down in excitement as if they had been apart for months. They were eighth graders. This was going to be the best year yet. They each felt something more grown-up and exciting about the first day of eighth grade, and they were ready for it.

With a few minutes to spare before the bell rang, the girls stopped and leaned against their tree for a quick survey of the school yard. It was easy to identify the sixth graders. They were nervous, furtively glancing in every direction, the most telltale sign of a sixth grader, and had new outfits and two-day-old haircuts. The girls easily but not fondly remembered how scary it was to be new to middle school and felt sorry for the new sixth graders.

The seventh graders were a little more confident but still not nearly cool enough to speak to the eighth graders. Most students, no matter their grade, carried backpacks, and some had musical instruments. Some even had new glasses or had discarded their glasses in favor of contacts.

"Look over there." Kelly pointed across the grassy lawn to a student. A new student, obviously a sixth grader, struggled with his backpack and what appeared to be a saxophone case. Two bigger boys, eighth graders, grabbed the case out of his hands and held it over his head. They teased him mercilessly until the bell rang, forcing them to abandon their fun and head into the school. The girls shook their heads and sighed—some things never changed—as they began to walk toward the doors.

Kelly and Sam both stopped to reach into their backpacks to turn off their new cell phones before entering the school—it would make for a horrible first day of school if they were to get their phones taken away.

"You're so lucky," Macy whined as she watched Kelly flip open her shiny blue phone, which was carefully decorated with sparkly gems. Sam laughed and turned off her sporty red phone, slid the top closed, and dropped it into her bag. Macy's parents wouldn't let her have a cell phone until high school.

"When did you guys get cell phones?" Lindsay asked.

"I got mine yesterday, and Sam got hers on Saturday," Kelly explained. "My mom wanted to have a way to reach me in case of an emergency and for me to be able to reach her. I'm not supposed to use it just anytime I want to."

"Same with me. I might as well not have it. I can call anyone who has the same service or use it as much as I want to on nights and weekends, but that's it," Sam complained.

"It's still way more than I have. You're so lucky," Macy said emphatically.

Lindsay sighed and agreed with Macy while she smeared untinted lip gloss onto her lips. "I have no idea when I'll ever get to have a cell phone. My mom thinks that they are bad for 'kids.'" She rolled her eyes to accentuate the point that she not only thought she should have a cell phone but that she definitely disagreed with the labeling of herself and her friends as *kids*. "She won't even let me use colored lip gloss. She thinks I'm too young."

With their cell phones turned off, backpacks slung over their shoulders, lip gloss perfectly accenting their skin tanned by the lazy days of summer, and their arms locked, the four best friends were ready to enter the school to begin their eighth-grade year.

Seeing their reflection in the glass doors

of the school as they approached it, Lindsay noticed how tall they'd all become over the summer. Four pairs of new jeans, four similar T-shirts, and four long manes of shiny hair—they were similar in so many ways but different enough to keep things interesting.

Kelly Garrett was the leader of the group. The girls almost always looked to her to get the final word on anything from plans they might make, to boys they liked, to clothes they wore. She was a natural leader, which was great most of the time. Her strong opinions sometimes caused conflict, though. Sam Lowell, the comedienne of the group, was always looking for a way to entertain them and make them laugh. She was willing to try anything once, and her friends enjoyed testing her on that. Macy Monroe was the sweet one. She was soft-spoken and slow to speak. She hated to offend anyone and got her feelings hurt easily. Then there was Lindsay. She was in the middle, the glue. She was strong but kind and was known to be a peacemaker. She often settled disputes between the girls to keep them from fighting.

Amid complete chaos—students talking, locker doors slamming shut, high fives, and whistles—the first day of school began. There was an assembly for the eighth graders, so the four girls headed toward the gymnasium together rather than finding their separate ways to their first classes.

The girls filed into the bleachers together, tucking their belongings carefully beneath their feet so nothing would fall through to the floor below. The room was raucously loud as 150 eighth graders excitedly shared stories of their summers and reunited with friends.

The speakers squealed as the principal turned on his microphone and tried to get everyone's attention. "Welcome back to Central Middle School. Let's all stand together to recite the Pledge of Allegiance."

Conversations slowly trailed off to a dull roar as teachers attempted to create some order in each row. The eighth graders shuffled to their feet and placed their right hands over their hearts to recite the pledge. The principal began: "I pledge allegiance to the flag. . . ."

Lindsay joined in, but her mind wandered as she looked down the row at each of her best friends. She thought back over the great summer they had just enjoyed. Together, they had spent many days languishing in the hot sun by Kelly's pool. She remembered the day when Sam got a bad sunburn from lying on the tanning raft for hours and not listening to the girls when they suggested that she reapply her sunscreen. She had wanted a good tan, and she paid the price. Kelly had the bright idea of using olive oil and lemon juice to take away the sting—she thought she'd heard that somewhere—but all it did was make Sam smell bad for days, along with the suffering that her burns caused.

They also had gone shopping at the mall whenever Sam's mom would pile them into her SUV and drop them off for a few hours so they could check out the latest fashions and watch for new students—boys in particular. Their favorite mall activity was to take a huge order of cheese fries and four Diet Cokes to a table at the edge of the food court so they could watch the people walk by.

They had a blast burying each other in the sand at the beach whenever Macy's dad took a break from job hunting to spend the day lying in the sun. One time they even made a huge castle with a moat. The castle had steps they could climb, and the moat actually held water. It took them almost the entire day, but the pictures they took made it all worthwhile.

They had also shared a weeklong trip to Lindsay's Bible camp. It was a spiritual experience for Lindsay, who used the time to deepen her relationship with God. She enjoyed being able to bring her friends into that part of her life—even if it was just for a week. Macy, more than the others, showed some interest and said that she'd like to attend youth group with Lindsay when it started up again in the fall. All four girls enjoyed the canoe trips—even the one when the boat capsized and they got drenched. They swam in the lake and played beach volleyball. The week they spent at camp was a good end to what they considered a perfect summer.

Although there was a certain finality to their fun and freedom with the arrival of the school year, there was excitement, too, as they took this next step toward growing up together. Lindsay took a moment to imagine what it would be like in the future. In just one year they would start high school together. After several years, they would head off to the same college and room together, as the plan had always been. At some point, they would each find someone to settle down with and get married. They had already figured out who would be the maid of honor for whose wedding. That way they each got to do it once. And they would be bridesmaids for each other. Then they would have children. Hopefully they would have them at around the same time so their children could grow up together, too. Beautiful plans built on beautiful friendships. . .what more could a girl ask for?

". . .One nation, under God, indivisible, with liberty and justice for all." The Pledge of Allegiance ended, and all the students sat down to hear about the exciting new school year.

Chapter 2

THIS IS REAL WORK

Second period—the dreaded class two periods before lunch—seemed to drag on forever with lunch still two hours away and the day stretching on so long ahead of it. But not for Lindsay, Kelly, Macy, and Sam; they loved second period this year. Not only was it their favorite class—home economics—but it was also the only class that they all had together. It was like a little break in the day.

On the first day of school, Mrs. Portney, the much-loved home ec teacher, allowed them to break into groups of four. It would be in those groups that the class would work on cooking, sewing, and other craft projects. Of course, the Lindsay-Kelly-Macy-Sam group was a no-brainer, and the girls quickly arranged their seating so they could be together.

The first project for the class was to make a stuffed pillow—but not just any stuffed pillow. This one had to be special, unique, and creative. They were allowed to use felt, stuffing, and any other craft materials they wanted. Things like pipe cleaners, movable eyes, glitter, rhinestones, fabric markers, and stencils were all available to be used by the class. Or they could bring things from home to contribute to their project. They had ten minutes to put their heads together to decide what to make.

"What about a teddy bear pillow?" Lindsay suggested.

"No, someone makes that every year," Kelly said, shaking her head. "We want to do something really interesting."

"Hmm. How about a rainbow pillow?" Lindsay tried again.

"Nah, too boring," Sam replied.

"Oh! We could make a bicycle pillow with real wheels that spin." Macy suggested.

The girls laughed. "Who would want to lay on that?"

"We could do a big heart that says 'Macy loves Tyler' and put an arrow through it," Kelly teased Macy.

"Yeah, right." Macy laughed.

"I know!" Sam said, getting excited. "Why don't we do a Mrs. Portney pillow?"

The other girls just looked at her for a minute, not quite sure if she was serious or if she had lost her mind—or both.

"Well, we could make it really fluffy, just like Mrs. Portney. We'll put an apron on the pillow, just like the one Mrs. Portney wears. We'll give the pillow a cute pair of round glasses made out of felt and use a shiny fabric as the glass part."

"Yeah," Kelly jumped in, liking the idea and adding some suggestions. "We can put scissors, pencils, and a tape measure hanging out of her apron pocket."

"We'll put her in a navy blue dress just like the one that Mrs. Portney wears all the time," Macy added.

"And then," Lindsay jumped on board,

"we'll make it a gift to Mrs. Portney when we're done."

All four girls agreed that it was a winning idea, and they just couldn't wait to get started. They looked around the room and saw that the other groups were struggling over ideas and having a difficult time getting started.

"Class, when you have your ideas, please just write them down on a slip of paper, along with the names of the students who are in your group, and turn it in to me before class is over today."

"Uh, Mrs. Portney?" Sam hesitantly raised her hand.

"Yes, what is it, Samantha?" Mrs. Portney asked. She was the only teacher who didn't annoy Sam when she called her by her full name.

"Well, we were just wondering. . . ." Sam spoke for the group. "Can we keep our pillow idea a secret until we're done? It's kind of a surprise."

"Oh?" Mrs. Portney grinned at the possibilities and shifted her glasses down so she could peer at the four girls over the top of them. "I suppose that would be all right, even though it's highly unusual. But then again, what else should I expect from you four? As long as you understand that if you don't tell me what you're doing, I can't help guide you in the process. But even without my help, you're still responsible for every part of the project in order to get a full grade."

"No problem, Mrs. Portney. Thanks!"

The bell rang, and it was time to head off to their separate classes. Kelly had English, Macy had math, Lindsay went to social studies, and Sam headed off to PE.

"Ugh! What happened to summer?" Kelly lamented to her friends as they slumped toward the cafeteria for lunch after third period on Wednesday during the second week of school.

"I know exactly what you mean," Lindsay replied. "I thought they had to give you a few weeks before they started piling on the homework, but I think I already have two hours of homework for tonight, and the day is only half over."

"So much for eighth grade being so great,"

Sam laughingly agreed as she collapsed in her seat to eat her lunch.

"What's with you?" Lindsay asked Macy when she noticed that Macy had hardly said a word since they met up by their lockers a few minutes before.

"Oh, nothing really," Macy said unconvincingly. Her friends just looked at her, waiting, not about to let her off the hook that easily. "Well, it's just that my math class is much harder this year, and I barely made it through last year's class. My mom has been talking about a tutor, and I don't want to have to do that." She dejectedly slumped her shoulders and dropped her head onto her arms after pushing away her lunch tray.

"Can we help?" Lindsay offered. "We could help you study. I have the same class as you, and Kelly is ahead of both of us."

"Yeah," Kelly jumped in. "If all of us help, you should be able to pull out of this, no problem."

"I don't know." Macy wasn't convinced. "I already failed my first quiz. I just don't have a math brain, I guess. I think I'm prepared, but then the test starts, and I can't remember anything about the formulas and the order of the steps. You can help me study, but I think my memory is the problem. . .or something like that." Macy looked defeated, and no one quite knew what to say to help.

Changing the subject to take her friend's mind off her troubles, Sam jumped in with an idea. "I know!" she shouted.

Lindsay and Kelly were startled by her outburst and almost knocked over their drinks.

"What's gotten into you, silly?" Kelly asked, laughing.

"Well," Sam continued, "Saturday is only three days away. Let's have a sleepover at my house. We'll celebrate making it through the second week of school by eating some junk food, watching some movies, and staying up late. What do you say?"

"Oh, count me in!" Kelly jumped at the chance.

"Me, too!" Macy quickly added.

"Well, you guys know my mom won't let me stay out on a Saturday because of church on Sunday, so you'll have to count me out," Lindsay replied.

"Oh no!" Sam jumped in, shaking her head. She held up a finger so she could finish chewing her bite of food, swallowed, grabbed a quick drink of milk to wash it down, and said, "No way are we leaving you out. We'll do it Friday." To a chorus of agreement from the other girls, Lindsay agreed to the plans, and the girls were relieved to have something fun to look forward to.

"Now let's make a list," Macy, ever the planner, suggested, excited to be able to move on from the depressing talk of her math class. "What should we do, and what should we bring?"

"Definitely a movie," Kelly suggested.

"Okay. And we can't do a movie without a pizza." Macy wrote MOVIE and PIZZA on the list.

"What about a game?" Lindsay asked.

"Oh, girls, I have a game for us, but it's a surprise. You'll have to wait until Friday night to find out what it is," Sam teased.

"Sounds mysterious." Macy wrote down: SAM'S SECRET GAME. And all of the girls giggled. They made their plans for Friday night and agreed that it would be a nice diversion to what was shaping up to be a tough year.

Macy, who was watching her weight

as usual, picked the sausage and pepperoni off her pizza. Kelly, who never worried about her weight, silently reached over to grab Macy's pepperoni.

"Hey!" Macy smacked her hand away. "What are you doing?"

"Well, you're not going to eat them."

"No, but I'd rather not have it shoved in my face that you can eat anything you want and never gain weight!" Macy whined.

"My mom gets so mad when I talk about dieting or watching what I'm eating," Lindsay said. "She thinks we're too young to worry about it and that we should just enjoy being kids."

"No one wants to get fat," Kelly snorted. "And we aren't kids, but we aren't grown-ups yet either, so I'm not going to worry about it just yet."

"I agree that no one wants to be fat," Lindsay countered, "but we should be careful and think about what we eat because it's healthier, not so we can be skinny."

"Easy for you to say," Macy grumbled.

"I'm not skinny at all," Lindsay said defensively.

"No, not skinny, but you're not fat either. You're perfect."

"Oh, I don't feel perfect. I don't think anyone does," Lindsay explained. "I just think we should be able to relax about things a little more. There's too much pressure to be what other people want us to be. As long as we're happy about who we are inside, that should be enough for people to be friends with us, right?"

"It's not like it's something you have to choose between, Linds. I mean, we can be nice and skinny at the same time, right?" Sam was confused.

"Of course you can. I'm just talking about priorities. I don't want to be the kind of person who looks at someone's outside appearance and judges them on whether they're skinny enough or not."

"True," Sam agreed. "But unfortunately, not everyone feels that way. And for that reason, I'll stick to my salad and skip the french fries when we go out to eat."

"Yeah, and if you don't mind," Macy replied, still irritated, "I'll pick off my pepperoni if I want to."

"Okay, okay, okay." Lindsay gave in, laughing. "I was just trying to give us a new outlook. You guys are perfect in my book, no matter how you look."

Chapter 3

SLEEPOVER PARTY

"Mom, did you hear the doorbell ring?" Sam shouted excitedly, forgetting that her mom wasn't even home. She'd been waiting for her friends for what seemed like hours. Running to the front door, Sam swung it wide open to find Kelly and Macy. The three girls squealed in excitement, and Kelly turned to wave at her mom as she backed out of the driveway with a little honk. They all turned to look down the street, anxious because they couldn't get started without Lindsay. With Lindsay nowhere in sight, they dropped to the porch step to wait until she arrived.

"She's here! She's here!" the girls yelled

when Lindsay's mom pulled into the driveway to drop her off for the night.

"Hi, Mrs. Martin." Sam waved a greeting.

Mrs. Martin chuckled at the girls' excitement. "You girls see each other almost every single day. How can you get so excited over just one more day?"

"Oh, Mrs. Martin, this is different," Sam assured her. "This is a special night. It's our first sleepover as eighth graders."

"Well, all right." Mrs. Martin laughed and rolled her eyes. "Just be sure that you eighth graders stay out of trouble."

"We will," the girls promised.

"Now come on!" Sam linked arms with Kelly, Kelly grabbed Lindsay's arm, Lindsay grabbed Macy, and they all started to walk in together.

Mrs. Martin honked and waved. Through her open window, she reminded Lindsay, "You remember what I said—be good."

The girls walked together into the house, squealing and giggling all the way.

"What should we do first?" Kelly asked.

"My mom bought all the stuff for us to

31

make pizza, and she left instructions for us. She and Dad went to a friend's house for dinner and won't be home until later, so she thought that would be fun for us," Sam explained.

"Cool!" The girls agreed it would be fun to make their own pizza, and knowing how long things could take when they started messing around, they got started right away.

Looking at the list, Sam got out the ingredients. There was dough to unroll, sauce to spread, cheese to sprinkle, and, of course, pepperoni to put on top.

"Oops. . .we almost forgot. It says to preheat the oven to four hundred degrees," Sam told the girls.

"I'll get that," Lindsay said, since she was standing right in front of the oven. Sam dug out pizza pans, and the other girls washed their hands and rolled up their sleeves.

Pizza Instructions
1. *Preheat the oven to 400 degrees.*
2. *Spray the pizza pan with nonstick spray, and sprinkle with flour.*
3. *Spread the dough onto the pizza pan evenly.*

4. *Evenly apply the pizza sauce to cover the dough.*

5. *Sprinkle the cheese all over the pizza.*

6. *Spread the pepperoni on the top of the pizza.*

7. *Bake for approximately 15–18 minutes, checking it regularly.*

8. *Be careful when you take it out. It's going to be HOT!*

Lindsay said, "I'll do the spray."

"I'll sprinkle the flour," said Kelly. When it was her turn to sprinkle the flour, she got a mischievous look on her face and flicked her fingers at Lindsay and Sam, who were standing nearby.

"Hey!" The girls giggled as they shook their long hair over the sink to get the flour out.

Sam spread the sauce, and they all took turns sprinkling the cheese. They worked on spreading the pepperoni until the pizza was completely covered and then added a few more just to make sure. Into the oven it went.

Sam set the timer, and the girls turned to take a look at the kitchen that they needed to clean while the pizza cooked. It was a disaster! With a chorus of four loud groans, they started cleaning up their mess, wishing they hadn't been so sloppy while they prepared the pizza. They had to put all the ingredients away, clean up the dishes, wipe off the countertops, and clean the floor. Eventually, though, they had the kitchen restored to what they thought was its original condition. Sam's mom might disagree, but she would be satisfied with their efforts.

Since Sam's mom had picked up some movies for them from the rental store, they chose one to watch on Sam's huge plasma television screen while they ate their pizza, which had finished baking at almost the exact time that they finished their cleaning. Armed with plates piled high with pizza and cans of soda, they settled in on the big leather sofa in the basement to watch their movie.

After a little while, Sam nudged Lindsay. "Hey, look over there." Sam pointed to Kelly, who was sound asleep on the sofa. The girls giggled quietly.

"Hmm. . .what should we do to her?" Lindsay asked the girls—because, as everyone knew, the first person to fall asleep at a sleepover got pranked. It was usually Macy who fell asleep first, so the girls saw this as a unique opportunity to do something fun and sneaky to Kelly.

"We could fill her shoes with shaving cream," Sam suggested. The girls laughed but dismissed the idea because Kelly wouldn't discover it until the next morning, which would be no fun—plus they could get in trouble if her shoes got ruined. So, after conspiring together for a few minutes, they concocted a pretty devious plan that they were quite proud of.

Sam went to the kitchen to fill a glass with very cold water and even added a few ice cubes to it to make sure it was cold enough. They balanced the glass very carefully on the back frame of the couch, which was leaning against the wall, and then propped it there with the little decorative pillows that Sam's mom had sitting around on the sofa. They made sure that the only direction the glass could fall was forward. The three girls tiptoed to the door and quietly left the room. When they made it out the door, Sam reached back, took the doorknob, and pulled really hard.

Bam! The door slammed shut. The girls quickly opened the door just a crack so they could see the scene they had created.

With the slamming of the door, Kelly immediately woke up and looked around the room, half asleep and confused. Startled and seeing that she was alone, she sat up abruptly. The pillows supporting the water glass were disturbed, and the glass tumbled forward, drenching Kelly from her neck all the way down the front of her shirt with ice-cold water.

She squealed as the water touched her skin, sending shivers through her body and taking her breath away. Openmouthed and gasping for air, she looked around the room and saw no one there with her. For a second, she was angry, ready to take out her frustration on someone. Then she heard the girls trying really hard not to giggle, and even though she tried not to laugh, she couldn't help herself. When the other three saw that she was being a good sport, they tumbled through the door, laughing so hard they could barely stand up straight. Sam fell to the tiled basement floor in fits of laughter as Kelly grabbed a towel from the laundry pile to dry herself.

"It serves. . .you right. . .for falling asleep . . .so early!" Lindsay tried to talk in between gales of laughter.

"Okay, okay, I get it." Kelly gave in, shaking her head. "But you had all better be careful, because I am well rested now, and I'll be up long after all of you fall asleep." The girls laughed good-naturedly.

They carried their dishes and garbage upstairs to the kitchen so they could make sure everything was cleaned up before Sam's mom and dad got home.

"So, Macy. . . ," Kelly hesitantly began while they were straightening the kitchen.

"Yeah?" Macy waited for Kelly's question.

"What's the deal with you and Tyler Turner this year?"

The other two girls stopped what they were doing. Sam even turned off the water in the sink so she could hear Macy's reply.

"What are you talking about?" Macy asked innocently but smiled as she looked away.

"Oh no! Don't even think about pretending that you don't know what I'm talking about." Kelly wouldn't let her off the hook that easily.

"She's blushing!" Lindsay shouted when Macy's cheeks turned bright red.

"No, I'm not blushing," Macy insisted. "I'm just hot."

"Right! Sure!" The girls didn't believe her and continued demanding answers. "It's time to fess up," Lindsay insisted.

"All right, all right," Macy relented. "The thing is, I don't know what is going on with Tyler. I mean, you guys know that I've liked him forever—like, for two whole years. But I don't think he knows that I exist. But then sometimes it feels like he likes me, too."

"Right—I mean, how do you explain the fact that every time I leave my science class, he's there by your locker, waiting for you to come out of math? Hmm?" Kelly pried.

"He's just being nice," Macy insisted. She continued. "What do you think I should do? I mean, my parents probably wouldn't let me date anyway, so I guess it's all for the best."

"Here's what we'll do." Sam jumped in with an idea. "I'll ask his cousin Stephanie, whose brother, Kenny, is Tyler's best friend, if he likes you. But I won't tell her who wants to know."

Kelly and Lindsay loved the idea, but Macy was hesitant. "Oh, I don't know. . . ."

"Oh, you should totally do that. It's perfect," Kelly insisted.

"Okay," Macy agreed. "As long as he doesn't find out that you asked for me."

"Deal!" Sam assured her, and the girls high-fived each other.

They heard the garage door start to open. With a little squeal, they hurriedly put away the last item and rushed out of the kitchen, turning off the lights on their way out. Trying to avoid the parents, the girls rushed downstairs to the basement, where they planned to sleep all night. Sam's mom popped her head downstairs for a quick second just to let the girls know they were home and then headed upstairs to bed.

As soon as they heard the bedroom door close upstairs, Sam got a glimmer in her eye and began to look at the girls, one at a time, teasing them until they remembered.

"Oh!" Macy exclaimed, catching on. "Let's play Sam's secret game."

"We can do that. But only if you're sure you're ready...," Sam teased mysteriously. "There are some rules."

"We're ready," everyone agreed a bit hesitantly, wondering what Sam had cooked up for them this time.

Chapter 4

TRUTH OR DARE

"So?" Lindsay started. "Let's have it, Sam. What is this game you've kept such a secret all week?"

"Yeah, let's play," the other two girls chimed in.

"Well, if you're sure you want to play," Sam explained, "you have to really agree to play for real, no matter what. It's a matter of honor."

"How can we agree if we don't know what the game is?" Lindsay asked nervously.

"Well, all I can tell you until you agree is that the game is called Truth or Dare, and the key to it is that there are no limits. And you can't bail out."

"How do you play?" Kelly asked Sam.

"Yeah," Macy prodded. "You have to tell us the rules before we can agree to it."

"Me, too. No way am I agreeing without knowing what I'm agreeing to." Lindsay was emphatic.

"Well, basically it's like this: When it's your turn, you choose whether you want a truth or a dare," Sam explained. "If you choose Truth, you will be asked a question that you have to answer truthfully. You cannot back out if you don't like the question. If you choose Dare, then you will be given a task—or a dare—that you must complete. You can't just decide that it's too hard or too risky. You *have* to do it. If you're scared that you won't be able to follow through, then you shouldn't agree to play at all."

"You mean we can't set any limits ahead of time, like about things we aren't allowed to do?" Lindsay was pretty nervous about the rules of the game.

"Nope. If you're too scared about what your dare might be, then just choose Truth. What have you got to hide, anyway?" Sam laughed as she sat down on the carpet. She knew that

Lindsay had no deep, dark secrets.

"I'm in!" Kelly shouted, joining Sam on the floor.

"Count me in," Macy added, joining them to make a half circle, leaving room for Lindsay.

"Well, I guess I'll play." Lindsay was really unsure about the game but decided she'd give it a try.

"Great! Then I'll go first. I'll choose Truth to get us started," Sam said.

The other three girls went into the corner to whisper for a few minutes about what to ask Sam, who was waiting on the floor. Giggling, they returned to the circle and took their places. Since Lindsay was seated right next to Sam and it would be her turn next, she asked the question: "Sam, have you ever taken something that didn't belong to you? And we mean, since you've been older than, say, fifth grade," Lindsay clarified.

"Ooh, good question." Sam was impressed that the game had gotten off to a great start. The girls seemed to understand how it was meant to be played. After contemplating her answer, she replied, "Yeah, this one time in sixth grade, I really, really wanted this pack of stickers from the card store, and I decided to take them when my mom wasn't looking. When we got back into the car, she noticed them and made me return them. I got into a *lot* of trouble for that."

Laughing at Sam's story, the girls turned their attention to Lindsay who had to select a truth or a dare for her turn. Lindsay, becoming slightly more confident in the game, selected Truth, too. The three girls left Lindsay sitting on the floor while they discussed what they should ask her as her Truth question. It seemed to take a long time, and Lindsay began to impatiently pick at her nails while she waited for them. Finally they scurried back to the floor and resumed their spots in the circle.

Kelly, who was sitting next to Lindsay, got to ask the next Truth question. "Lindsay, your Truth question is: Do you ever hate going to church or resent that your parents make you go all the time?"

Lindsay hesitated over that one. She knew she had to tell the truth, but she also wanted to protect her witness and make sure she wasn't misrepresenting her feelings about God, her church, and her parents. . .but she had to tell the truth. "Well, it's not that I ever 'hate' going to church; I love my church. And I don't 'resent' my parents for making me go all the time. I know they just want what's best for me. But sometimes it's a drag to have to miss out on fun things and not be able to make plans several times a week because of church activities. Overall, though, I don't think I would trade it." Satisfied with her answer, she breathed a deep sigh of relief and felt that her honesty probably did more good for her cause than hurt it.

Kelly's turn. "I pick Dare!"

"How did I guess?" Macy laughed. The girls eagerly got up from the floor, letting Kelly wait there patiently while they decided what she was to do for her dare. There were lots of whispers and giggles coming from the other side of the room, which made Kelly squirm nervously, a bit afraid of what she'd gotten herself into. After waiting for about five minutes, she called over to the girls, "Come on now, this is the first dare. Go easy."

After a few more minutes, the girls came rushing back to the floor and resumed a lopsided, halfhearted circle. Macy couldn't wait to tell Kelly what her dare was. She informed Kelly that she had to sneak upstairs into Sam's brother's room and take his baseball cleats while he was sleeping in the room and then soak them in water and put them in the freezer!

"Oh man! You girls are rotten." Kelly laughed but immediately rose to begin her dare.

She crept up the stairs with the other girls following her and paused in front of the closed bedroom door. Kelly took a deep breath and then slowly pushed it open. They could see the rise and fall of the covers on the bed as Sam's brother breathed deeply in his sleep. Kelly carefully opened the door a little more so she could get into the room without making a noise. It squeaked a little bit when she pushed on it, but Sam's brother didn't wake up or even stir.

Kelly made her way across the room, stepping over a soccer ball, two pair of shoes, a couple of piles of clothes, and some magazines. When she got near the bed, she looked around the room and finally spotted the baseball cleats. They were hanging on a peg right above the headboard of the bed on the opposite side.

She looked back at the girls in the doorway, who were trying really hard not to laugh out loud. Nearing the bed, she tried to hold her breath so she would make less noise. Slowly she leaned across the bed, being very careful not to touch it or slip and fall onto it. The thought of that paralyzed her for a moment as she imagined falling on top of Sam's brother and him waking up. Shaking her head to clear the thought, she knew that no matter what she couldn't let that happen. So she firmly planted her feet and reached across the bed toward the cleats hanging on the wall across from her.

She couldn't reach them!

Hearing muffled giggles from the hallway, she shot an angry look at the girls, telling them to be quiet. Kelly backed up a little bit and looked for something she could use to unhook the shoes from their peg.

Aha! She spotted a pair of crutches that Sam's brother had to use when he hurt his ankle a few months ago. Taking one of the crutches, she silently lifted the crutch and pointed it toward the baseball cleats. She leaned in slowly and carefully until the bottom of the crutch was hooked into the tied-together laces of the cleats. She slowly lifted the crutch and freed the cleats from their perch on the peg, turning carefully so that the cleats were no longer hanging over the bed. Bending slowly to the floor, Kelly laid everything down onto the floor and then stepped over to grab the cleats and put the crutch back where she found it.

After creeping out of the room and closing the door behind her, the girls all ran to the kitchen and collapsed into fits of laughter. Kelly was out of breath and all wound up and shaking due to her nerves.

But her dare wasn't quite over, the other girls reminded her.

Looking in the kitchen cabinets, Kelly found an old pot that she filled with water. After hesitating for just a moment, she dropped the shoes into the water. Sam cleared a place in the freezer, and Kelly put in the pot. Then they scurried back down to the basement where they laughed so hard they had to wipe tears from their eyes. "Boy, I sure hope he doesn't have a baseball game tomorrow," Kelly said.

"It's not baseball season, anyway," Macy reminded them. "I just hope he finds them before Sam's mom does."

The thought of Sam's mom opening the

freezer in the morning to find a pot of shoes inside started the giggles all over again.

Macy's turn.

"Oh man, I'm scared to pick Dare," Macy admitted.

"Go for it. We've had two Truths already," the other girls encouraged her.

"Okay, let's get it over with," Macy giggled. "I pick Dare."

The three girls rushed over to the corner to discuss what the dare should be. Almost immediately, Sam rushed over to the desk in the corner and grabbed the phone book. They tore through it until they found what they're looking for. Scribbling furiously on a piece of paper, they start to giggle.

Uh-oh, Macy thought. *What have I gotten myself into?*

When they got back to the circle, Kelly thrust a scrap of paper at Macy. Macy was confused when she saw that a phone number had been hastily scribbled on the paper. "Whose number is this, and what am I supposed to do with it?"

Kelly explained, "You need to call that

number, and when the machine picks up, say, 'This is Macy Monroe. Can you come out to play?' And then hang up."

"That sounds simple enough, but whose number is it, and what if they answer?"

"Mace, we're not going to tell you whose number it is—that's part of the dare. And if they answer, you still have to say it. But they probably won't answer. It's almost two in the morning."

"Okay, let's just do this." Macy couldn't wait to get it over with, so she immediately began to dial the phone. Sam reached over to put the phone on speaker so they all could hear. It rang three times and then a fourth time, when the answering machine finally picked up.

"Hello, you've reached the Turner residence." Macy's eyes got really wide; she gasped and started to panic. ". . .No one is available to answer your call right now. . .please leave a message after the beep."

"Um. . .hello. . .this is Macy. . . . Um. . . can you. . .um. . .come out to play?" And then she hung up, embarrassed and red faced. The other three girls were laughing uncontrollably and rolling on the floor.

Macy, trying to be a good sport by pretending it was no big deal, shrugged and said, "Okay, now what?" The other three knew she was bluffing, and that made them laugh even harder.

"What? It's no big deal. I don't care." Macy tried to get them to believe it.

"Riiiight, like it doesn't bother you at all. You got sick to your stomach, and we all know it," Kelly teased.

"Well, how would you like to embarrass yourself like that? It wasn't fun, that's for sure."

"It was kind of fun for us." Sam laughed, and the others agreed.

"So, judging by the yawns that have been going around the circle, I'd say it's time to get some sleep. What do you think?" Sam asked the group.

They'd had way more than enough fun for one night but agreed they would definitely play Truth or Dare again. They got out their toothbrushes and blankets and got ready for bed. Once settled, it still took them over an hour to actually stop chatting and fall asleep, but eventually they all dozed off with smiles on their faces.

Chapter 5

SUNDAY SCHOOL

"Rise and shine!" Lindsay's mom called from the doorway, letting her know it was time to get up and get ready for church.

"Ugh. Mom, can I just sleep in this one time? Please?" Lindsay groaned. "I promise I'll go next week."

"Oh no. You know better than that, young lady. We always go to church as a family, and this week will be no different."

Lindsay pulled the covers over her head and stopped short of saying something to her mom that she might live to regret.

"Breakfast is in fifteen minutes," Lindsay's

mom said as she left the room.

She knew that there was no way out of it. She also knew that if she let her mom know just how tired she was, Lindsay wouldn't be allowed to do sleepovers with the girls anymore, especially if it interfered with church. She slowly sat up and let her eyes grow accustomed to the bright sunshine that filled her room. Sleepily she made her way to the bathroom in the hallway, where she brushed her teeth and her hair—grateful that she had taken a shower the night before—and splashed water on her face. Lindsay applied just the barest hint of makeup, hoping it would help liven her face and keep her from looking so tired.

Shuffling back to her bedroom, she pulled open her closet door and began to sort through her dresses and skirts, looking for an outfit that would perk her up. Finding just the perfect thing, Lindsay slipped into a light brown skirt cut just above the knee—almost too short for her mom's taste—and a cute denim top. On her way out of the room, she stopped in front of the mirror and clipped her hair back on one side with a silver butterfly clip, sprayed on a squirt of perfume, and, satisfied with the finished product, headed downstairs with two minutes to spare.

"Well, there she is," Mom said in her usually cheery voice.

"I was thinking we'd have to send in the troops to drag her out," Lindsay's dad added.

Rolling her eyes and laughing, Lindsay reached for her plate and took a spoonful of scrambled eggs and two pieces of bacon.

"Father," her dad began to pray, "please bless this food and nourish our bodies and our souls today. We give this day to You to use for Your glory. Amen." Lindsay and her mom added their amens and began to eat.

On the way to church, Lindsay's mom turned in her seat so that she could see Lindsay. "So, how was Friday night over at Sam's? What did you girls do all night?"

"Oh, it was fun. We stayed up kind of late and talked and played some games."

"What kind of games did you play?" Mrs. Martin pressed uncharacteristically.

"Oh, nothing really, just some different games and one that Sam made up." Lindsay wondered what her mom was getting at—this line of questioning seemed a little out of the ordinary.

"Well, I got a call from Mrs. Lowell, Sam's mom. It seems that she got up this morning and went to make some breakfast. She was surprised to find something in the freezer. What do you suppose she found there, Linds?"

"It was just a dare that Kelly had to do. She. . .um. . .well, you probably already know what she had to do," Lindsay stammered, trying not to laugh.

"Yes, it appears that she put Scott Lowell's baseball shoes in a pot of water and froze them," her mom said sternly.

Even from her spot in the backseat, Lindsay could see that her dad was trying very hard not to laugh—and he was losing the battle.

"Whatever possessed you girls to do that?" Mrs. Martin asked.

"Oh, come on," Lindsay's dad jumped in. "It's just a harmless prank. We all did things like that. It's a pretty clever one, too, if you ask me."

Relieved that she had her dad on her side, Lindsay looked back at her mom, who was carefully choosing her next words.

"Lindsay, I just want you to be aware that harmless pranks can still be costly to people and cause harm. Also, one harmless prank often leads to another until, before you know it, you're trapped into doing something that never would have happened if you hadn't gone down that road to begin with. Do you know what I'm saying, sweetie?"

"Yeah, Mom, I get it. I'll be careful. I promise."

"Just keep in mind what I said. Damage can be done even when you think it's perfectly harmless."

As soon as the car pulled into the church parking lot, Lindsay jumped out and ran ahead to join her youth group friends on the lawn, before another word could be said about the sleepover.

"Would you all please stand for the reading of God's Word?" Pastor Tim paused to wait for the congregation to rise to their feet. "Today's reading will be taken from the book of First Thessalonians, chapter 5." He read to them from the Bible, and then they were all seated for the sermon.

In his sermon, Pastor Tim showed how the Bible warned Christians to avoid even the appearance of evil. "Think about what that means and why we would need a warning like that. I mean, sin is sin, right? Appearing to sin isn't the same thing as actually doing it, is it? So why would we be warned in scripture to avoid even looking like we are involved in evil things? I'll tell you why. It's because God asks us to be His ambassadors. He calls us to bring the light of His love to this dying world. How can we possibly do that if we are involved in things that appear to be evil or sinful? Whether we're guilty or not doesn't matter at that point. All that matters is that when a Christian seems to be doing wrong, he is assumed to be a hypocrite, and Christianity suffers. Satan just waits for Christians to make mistakes—or, in the case of what we're talking about today, to even appear to make mistakes. Then he can capitalize on those mistakes and use them against the cause of Christ.

"So take care not to find yourself in questionable situations. One way to do this is to really think and pray about the people you consider to be your friends. As my mother always told me, 'You are known by the company you keep.' That means that what your friends are known for, you will be known for, too. If your friends are known for questionable behavior, it will be assumed that you condone and participate in it.

"Also, we are all susceptible to the effects of temptation. Sin creeps in slowly and grabs hold of us before we even realize it. Your intentions can be completely pure, but over time the line between what is right and what is wrong becomes fuzzy. Eventually, if you allow yourself to be exposed to sinful behavior, it won't seem so bad and you'll forget your resolve, giving in to temptation and peer pressure. Think of it like a dark mist that slowly engulfs you. At first, you barely see the mist, but eventually you can barely see anything else because of it."

Lindsay sat next to her parents and thought hard about what Pastor Tim was saying. She was grateful for her friends and that they were good girls. But being in eighth grade and knowing that high school was right around the corner, Lindsay promised herself it was advice that she would follow.

Pastor Tim closed the service, and everyone stood up to leave. On their way out, Lindsay's mom and dad stopped to talk to several friends. Knowing that it would take them a long time to make their way to the car, Lindsay went to see if she could find any of her youth group buddies. She headed over to the new addition to the church that was still under construction. Pulling back the plastic that hung as a divider between the current church and the new building, she stepped in among the dust and tools to see if anyone was hanging out in there. It had become the typical place for teens to go during the church service to hang out when they didn't want to actually sit through the service.

"Hey, you guys! What's up?" Lindsay asked the three teens she found back there.

Scott, Tanner, and Christy had seen someone coming and were scurrying to hide something. When they saw that it was Lindsay, they relaxed a little bit.

"What are you guys doing back here?" Lindsay asked.

"Oh, we're just hanging out, chatting, you

know," Tanner answered.

"Okay, fine, don't tell me what's really going on." Lindsay laughed, knowing that there was more to the story.

"Lindsay, if you promise not to say anything, I'll show you." Christy pulled out a pack of cigarettes and a lighter from behind her back. "Want one?"

Thinking back to Pastor Tim's sermon, Lindsay realized that if someone happened upon them at just that moment, Lindsay would immediately appear just as guilty as the others. She hadn't smoked the cigarettes, and she didn't even think it was okay that the others had. But still, it would be assumed that she was involved in it or at least condoned the behavior just because she was hanging out with them. She knew that her best bet was to get out of there right away.

"Uh, no thanks. I really need to get going." Lindsay left immediately and went to find her parents, grateful for the real-life sermon illustration to drive home the point of what she had learned.

Lindsay could hear her computer chirping for her the instant they entered the house after having lunch with some of her parents' friends after church. She was getting instant messages, and lots of them. Rushing to her room, she saw her messenger program lit up like a Christmas tree. Sam, Kelly, and Macy were all online and trying to get her to show up for a chat session. Knowing that these chat sessions could take hours, Lindsay ran to get a can of soda before she settled in and let them know she was there.

"Linds," her mom called, hearing her in the kitchen, "if you're planning to get on the computer, you only have about thirty minutes before we head over to your grandma's—don't forget."

"No problem, Mom," Lindsay replied, not letting her mom know that she had, in fact, forgotten about the visit.

Rushing back to her room, Lindsay plopped down into her chair and typed a message to the group. *I'm here!* she typed.

Macy: *Hi, stranger!*

Kelly: *Where've u been?*

Lindsay: *Church, just got home, and I have to leave in 30. So what's up?*

Sam: *Kelly has a plan. She's just getting ready to tell us.*

Lindsay: *Cool! What is it?*

Kelly: *The other night was a blast, right?*

Lindsay: *Oh yeah!*

Macy: *Total blast!*

Sam: *Definitely!*

Kelly: *So let's make it a tradition. Let's have a sleepover every Friday at a different house.*

Macy: *I'm in!*

Sam: *Me, too, probably. I'll have to ask my mom; she's still kind of mad about the shoes. I guess my brother thinks he should get new shoes out of the deal.*

Macy: *lol*

Kelly: *LOL! Just give her some time. She'll be ready by the time it's your turn again. What do you say, Linds?*

Lindsay: *Oh sure, count me in!*

Sam: *So whose house is next, then?*

Macy: *I'll go next. My dad's going to be out of town this weekend, so my mom won't mind having us there.*

Lindsay: *Sounds good to me.*

Kelly: *Okay, then I'll go next.*

Sam: *Great!*

Lindsay: *After Kelly is my turn.*

Kelly: *Perfect! And we can play our game every time. It will be our tradition.*

Lindsay: *Didn't we cause enough trouble last time?*

Macy: *Yeah! I still can't look Tyler Turner in the eye!*

Sam: *And my mom was really mad about the shoes.*

Kelly: *That's part of the game. It's a risk. That's what makes it fun. We can make a rule that nothing we do can be destructive to anyone's property. How about that?*

Lindsay: *I think that def. should be the rule!*

Sam: *I agree.*

Macy: *Definitely!*

Lindsay: *Sounds like a plan. I have to run!*

Macy: *C U later!*

Kelly: *C U guys tomorrow!*

Sam: *Bye!*

After signing off her instant messenger program, Lindsay paused for a moment and considered the message of Pastor Tim's sermon this morning: Sin is slow; it creeps in like a dark mist, and you don't realize it until it engulfs you and everything around you until you can't see anything clearly. *I hope that doesn't ever happen to me.* But why worry? Everything was great. There was nothing to be concerned about.

Chapter 6

HOSTESS MACY

"What time should we be at your house tonight, Macy?" Lindsay asked, referring to the sleepover party they had planned for that night.

"Oh, anytime after five would be fine, I think. My dad is leaving for his trip this morning, and Mom likes to be home when I have friends over, as you all already know," Macy replied, rolling her eyes.

"Yeah, my parents are like that, too," Lindsay replied just as the bell rang, which signified that class was about to begin.

"Good morning, boys and girls," Mrs. Portney began the class. "Go ahead and get your projects out of your bins." One student from each group shuffled toward the bank of yellow bins in the cupboards on the wall where they had stored their project materials, notes, and scraps between classes. The bin for each group was clearly labeled with the names of each group and what they had chosen to make—except for Lindsay, Kelly, Sam, and Macy's bin. On theirs, it only said their names because of the special permission to keep their project a secret until it was finished.

The big yellow bins were placed on the tables in front of the group members, and the students awaited further instructions.

"Class," Mrs. Portney said, "I'd like for you to take a moment to make notes in your project notebook of what supplies and materials you've used and exactly how much you think you will use to complete the project. Then estimate the total cost of materials for your project. You can designate a group secretary for note-taking and then go ahead and get started. There is a supply list in the notebook on the front table if you need to consult it for names and prices of goods that have been provided to you. If there is something you have brought from home and you don't know the price, make an estimate and then write a question mark next to it so that we will know later on that it was only an estimate."

The girls took a look inside their bin and removed their materials from the brown paper bags. They spread out the piles of felt that they intended to use to make the body and the clothes, the aluminum foil for the eyeglasses, the movable eyes they would affix to Mrs. Portney's face, and all of the other supplies that they had contributed but weren't yet sure they would use.

"Mrs. Portney?" Lindsay raised her hand.

"Yes, Ms. Martin," Mrs. Portney responded.

"What about the things that we have in our bins that we aren't sure we'll use on our pillows? Should we include those things on the list?"

"Ah, good question. Yes, please include everything that you think you may use, and estimate prices like I've explained already. When the project is over, you'll be making a new list and comparing it to the old list—just for fun—to see how closely they match."

The students all nodded, understanding what they were to do. The four girls spread their supplies out into piles. They began the list, and

Lindsay agreed to act as group secretary and record the data. They spent the rest of the class period getting their supplies figured out and planning ahead for what they wanted to do with their project. They had to be very careful that the other students didn't overhear them talking. Since the girls' pillow project was a secret, the other students were desperately trying to figure it out and went so far as to beg the girls to let them in on the secret. The girls were holding out, though. They vowed not to tell a single person what their pillow was going to be.

Engrossed in their project, the bell rang before any of them realized that class was about to end. They hastily cleaned up their workstation, returned their bin to the appropriate shelf on the wall, and headed off to their respective classes.

"See you at lunch!" they shouted to each other as they raced in separate directions down the hall.

"Mom, I'm leaving for Macy's house," Lindsay called up the stairs when she saw Kelly's mom pull into the driveway to pick her up. She heard some quick rustling, and her mom came bounding down the stairs, making sure she didn't miss Lindsay's exit.

"Now, Linds, let's not have a repeat of last time, okay?" her mom cautioned.

"Don't worry, Mom. We've agreed that there can be no destruction of private property during our sleepovers." Lindsay laughed.

Mrs. Martin, not finding the comment very funny, became a bit more stern and said, "Lindsay, I am not kidding. You think before you act and be an example to your friends. Okay?"

"Yeah, Mom. I get it. I'll behave," Lindsay promised as Kelly's mom honked her horn. "Gotta go, Mom. Love you." Lindsay gave her mom a quick kiss and was out the door before Mrs. Martin could say another word. With a bounce in her step, she skipped off to the waiting SUV.

When Lindsay and Kelly arrived at Macy's house, they had to wait a moment before pulling into the driveway because Sam's mom was backing out. Kelly's mom rolled into the driveway, and the girls hopped out, grabbing their sleeping bags and pillows as they went.

"Bye, Mom!" Kelly shouted as she closed her door. Her mom nodded and waved as she backed out of the driveway and drove off. The girls rushed up to the door, which was propped open, waiting for them. Slowly, Lindsay pushed it open just a bit more and looked inside. They assumed that Macy and Sam saw them pulling in, so they didn't bother to ring the doorbell. But Lindsay wondered where they had taken off to.

"Hello?" Lindsay tentatively stepped into the house.

"Anyone there?" Kelly stepped in behind her.

"*Roar!*" Sam and Macy jumped at the other two girls from behind the half wall where they were hiding. Lindsay and Kelly both squealed in shock and then laughed at the silliness. When their heart rates recovered, Lindsay grabbed Macy and Kelly caught Sam, and they tickled the girls until they cried for mercy.

"So what are we going to do first?" Kelly asked when they had all recovered and caught their breath.

"My mom said she'd drop us off at the movie theater if we want to go," Macy replied.

"Hey, that's a great idea," Lindsay responded. "I'm all for that."

"Me, too," Kelly and Sam agreed simultaneously.

The girls opened the newspaper to the movie section and spread it out on the kitchen table so they could select the movie that they wanted to see. It only took a moment to decide because they had already seen two of the options together, so those were naturally out. Several of the other movies had ratings that the girls weren't allowed to watch. With two movies left to choose from—a cowboy movie or a romantic comedy—they decided on the comedy. They had an hour before they needed to leave, so they started getting ready.

All four girls crammed into Macy's tiny but private pink bathroom to get ready to go to the movies. Amid their piles of makeup, hairbrushes, earrings, and perfume, they treated the outing as if they were headed to the prom—"You never know who you might run into," they always said. Sam felt unprepared because she hadn't brought anything special to wear. Undaunted, the girls saw that as an opportunity to plow through

Macy's closet in efforts to find something for Sam to wear. They tried several things, but they were all too big for Sam's slight frame. "Okay, okay," Macy gave in. "I have a new shirt that I've been saving for when I lose ten more pounds on my diet. I haven't even taken the tags off it yet. You can wear it if you want to, Sam."

"Really?" Sam squealed. "Are you sure?" Macy assured Sam that she didn't mind and reached far back into her closet to find the shirt. She pulled out a cute little long-sleeved red top with silver buttons down the front and little pockets on the chest. Excitedly, Sam tried it on, and it fit perfectly.

"That movie was funny!" The girls all agreed as they laughed and bumped into each other coming out of the theater. They giggled as their eyes adjusted to the light, and they headed toward the food court. The movie ended at eight thirty, but they asked Macy's mom not to pick them up until nine thirty so they would have some time to hang out in the mall. With one order of french fries smothered in cheddar cheese and a diet cola to share, they chose their favorite seat on the edge of the food court so they could watch the people go by.

"So, Sam," Macy casually asked, "did you ever ask Tyler's cousin to ask Kenny if he liked me?"

"Oh! I totally forgot to tell you this," Sam was excited to report. "I did ask her. She talked to Kenny, and Kenny didn't even have to ask Tyler about you. Kenny told Stephanie that Tyler talks about you all the time and that he has for what seems like years. Kenny also said that he's been trying to get Tyler to make a move forever but that Tyler's just been too shy. What do you think about that?"

Macy tried not to make a big deal out of it, but she couldn't help the grin that quickly spread across her face. "I guess we'll just have to wait and see what happens, then."

"Just see what happens? Are you kidding me?" Kelly was so excited. "You might be the first one of us ever to have a boyfriend. We have to figure out a way to push that boy along a little."

"No, no. I don't want to push him along,

because I don't really know what I'm ready for. I mean, what am I going to do? Push him to ask me out only to have to tell him that I can't date? I would be so embarrassed," Macy explained. "I'm just happy to know that he is as interested in me as I am in him. If it took another year to act on it, that would be fine with me."

"I think that's the right way to look at it, Mace," Lindsay said.

"I guess I agree, even though I don't really like it." Sam pouted.

"I totally disagree," Kelly emphatically said. "I think that where there's a will, there's a way. And you'll regret it if you don't pursue this, Macy."

"Well, like I said, it really doesn't matter because he hasn't asked me out, and even if he did, I couldn't go." Macy sighed. "Let's just give it some time and see what happens."

The girls gathered in a circle on the floor for another game of Truth or Dare. This time Lindsay was first. She picked Truth again, and the other three girls groaned.

"Come on, Linds, you have to take a chance in life. What fun is it to do the same thing over and over?" Kelly prodded her.

"Yeah," Macy agreed. "You need to walk on the wild side now and then."

"Well, I'll pick Truth this time, but if we play again, I promise I'll pick Dare," Lindsay said, taking the chance and hoping that there might not be a next time.

"Okay." Sam gave in. "As long as you promise. It's no fun for us if you're going to play it safe every time."

"I promise."

"Well then, girls, let's go come up with a good Truth for Lindsay."

The three girls left Lindsay to sit in the circle while they discussed what to ask her for her Truth. While she waited, Lindsay wondered if she was getting herself into a mess. Maybe by giving them a whole week to come up with a good dare, she'd find herself in even more of a predicament than she would have if she had just done it right then. *Oh well*, she decided, *it's too late to worry about that now. It'll be okay.* . . . She hoped.

The girls ran back to the floor and dove into their spots. Since Sam was next in the circle, she got to ask Lindsay her Truth question. "Lindsay, which of the three of us do you like the best?"

"Oh come on!" Lindsay wailed. "You can't seriously expect me to answer that."

"Oh yes, you have to answer," Kelly replied. "You didn't think we'd make it easy for you, did you?"

Macy just looked on with a nervous expression on her face. "No one will be upset by your answer, Lindsay. But you do need to answer. It's part of the game."

"Fine. You guys asked for it." Lindsay was a little frustrated and figured that they deserved it if they didn't like her answer. "I'll have to say that my answer is Macy. She is the one I've known the longest, and her parents and my parents have been friends for decades. She understands and supports my religion and church commitments, and she deals with the same kind of rules from her parents as I do," Lindsay answered but cut Kelly off before she could interrupt.

"But. . .I'm not finished. Kelly and Sam,

you two are my best friends on an equal level with Macy. I could have gone my whole life without answering that question. Since I had to, those were the reasons I chose. I love you all equally, though. *There,* are you happy?"

The three girls collapsed into fits of giggles. They found it amusing that Lindsay was so worried about answering the question. Sam assured her that they knew how she would answer and that it was a logical and fair answer. Kelly pretended that she was crying and wiped her eyes, just to get to Lindsay. "It's not like we really care who your favorite is anyway, Lindsay," Kelly said sarcastically and then smiled when she saw the worried expression on Lindsay's face. "Oh, come on now. I'm just kidding."

"Now it's Sam's turn," said Macy, obviously wanting to change the subject.

"I choose Dare. Judging from Lindsay's question, Truth is no easier than Dare." Sam laughed.

Lindsay, Macy, and Kelly rushed off to come up with a good dare for Sam. They whispered for a few moments, but it didn't take them long. They came back to the circle and told

Sam what her dare was.

"Oh, that's no problem at all." Sam jumped up to perform her dare, and the other three looked a little disappointed that she didn't seem to mind it a bit.

Sam went upstairs to Macy's kitchen and, carefully, so that she didn't wake anyone up, took everything out of the kitchen cabinets and put it all neatly back into different cabinets. The glasses that had originally been right next to the sink were moved to the little cabinet over the refrigerator. The plates and bowls that had once been housed over the kitchen counter had switched places with the pots and pans.

Lindsay, Kelly, and Macy watched her in action, giggling. Well, Lindsay and Kelly were giggling, anyway. Macy knew that she'd be the one to have to put it all back the way it had been as soon as her mom tried to find something the next day. But she finally found the humor in the situation when she imagined her mom opening the cabinet to get a coffee cup and finding the blender instead.

"Macy's turn!" Kelly exclaimed as soon as they arrived downstairs after Sam completed the kitchen cabinet dare.

"I pick Dare," Macy said confidently.

"We already know what your dare is, Mace," Lindsay said smugly—they had already conspired to create a good dare for Macy.

"Oh no...what have I gotten myself into?" Macy wailed. "Is it too late to change to Truth?"

"Of course it is." Sam laughed.

Kelly explained Macy's dare to her. "You have to go over to the phone right now and dial Tyler Turner's house. When someone answers or if the answering machine picks up, you have to read what's on this piece of paper. But you can't look at it until it's time to read it."

Macy slumped to the floor in desperation. Having had a crush on Tyler for so long, the thought of embarrassing herself in front of him just made her stomach queasy. "Okay, I'll do it." She crept to the phone and picked up the receiver. As slowly as possible, she dialed the phone and waited for someone to pick up. The answering machine picked up, and Kelly handed her the slip of paper right before the beep.

"Hi, this is Macy calling. I was wondering if Tyler would like to"—Macy gulped and paused before she continued reading—"go on a date with me." She hastily hung up the phone almost in tears from embarrassment. "How am I ever going to face him?" Macy wailed at the girls who couldn't hear her over their own laughter.

When they had finally stopped laughing and Macy had time to think about what she had just done, she complained to the girls. "You guys! I asked you to leave it alone for a while and just wait to see what happens. He's going to think I'm asking him out on a date. And what if he responds that he wants to go out with me? What do I do then?"

"Just take it one thing at a time. It'll be okay, Macy. We just did you a favor. You'll see," Sam promised. After that dare, they admitted that they were tired but had one more Truth or Dare to administer. It was Kelly's turn. "I'm going to pick Truth this time."

Lindsay, Macy, and Sam conferred for a quick minute about what to ask Kelly. Nothing seemed to faze Kelly, so it was tough to come up with a question that would be difficult for her to answer. At Lindsay's prodding, they agreed to go another route on her behalf.

"Kelly," Lindsay began, "you must answer the following question truthfully. Do you already know what dare you will give to me next time, and will it be something horrible?"

Kelly shook her head and laughed. "Okay, you guys took the tired and easy way out, but that's fine. Um. . .yeah. . .I already know what I'll recommend. And, yeah, it will be horrible for you, Linds, but oh so much fun for us." Kelly grinned wickedly at the thought, while Lindsay wondered yet again what she had gotten herself into.

Chapter 7

YOUTH GROUP

Flames were visible through the trees as Lindsay and her dad pulled into the church parking lot just before the start of the first youth group session after the summer break. Knowing that there would be a bonfire that night, Lindsay had planned ahead by bringing a blanket to sit on, a jacket in case it got cool, and some snacks to share with the group. She wore her favorite designer jeans—she only owned one pair of true designer jeans, unlike many of her friends who had several, if not many, pairs—and her best cropped sweater over a white satin cami. Getting out of the car, she felt like a fashionista as she grabbed her things and, as an afterthought, reached into the back to get her Bible just in case she needed it.

"Bye, Dad! I'll see you at nine."

As her dad backed out of the parking lot, Lindsay took off for the tree line, toward the flames that rose higher and higher as the youth leaders fed more wood into the fire, getting it to roar.

"Hey, guys, need some help?" Lindsay called over to the guys working on the fire as she approached the clearing.

"Whooo-hoooo!" One of them whistled as she approached. "Summer was good to you, Linds."

Lindsay saw that it was Rob calling out to her. He was one of her church buddies whom she'd known since she was four. "Ha, ha, funny, Rob." Lindsay assumed he was teasing her.

"I'm serious, Linds; you look great," Rob continued.

"Well, thanks," Lindsay replied, her cheeks reddening from sudden embarrassment caused by the attention, half wishing she had worn a different outfit but secretly pleased with herself for her choice. She jumped in to help with the setup and got the firewood stacked up and ready to be added to the fire as needed, hoping to avoid any further comments or attention about her appearance.

When it was time to begin, the youth minister, Pastor Steve, took out his guitar to begin the worship time. As the music started, everyone grabbed a seat around the fire. Some sat on the ground; some sat on blankets they had brought from home. Lindsay perched atop a tree stump. Pastor Steve sat on a log and began to lead the group in some of the fun, rousing choruses that they learned at camp that summer and then some deeper, more soulful choruses to lead them into worship. The music went on for almost an hour but seemed to come to an end fast because of the atmosphere and the feelings of unity and friendship they all felt.

"Let's take this time to share some testimonies of how God blessed us or worked through us this summer," the youth minister suggested after the worship time wound down. "Who would like to go first? How about you, Rob? Would you like to share with us about what you did this summer?"

"Sure," Rob excitedly agreed. "I spent about six weeks traveling with a medical missions team through Mexico. It was amazing in so many ways. I wouldn't trade the experience for anything, and I can't wait to do it again.

"In specific, I came in contact with hundreds of kids. They were all very sick and needed to be taught better hygiene, better nutrition, and how to use the medications that we provided. There were so many children and adults who needed to be seen that there was no way for the doctors to see them all, so I had to see patients as if I were a doctor. I learned about what to look for and what medication to give, and I would share it with a doctor or nurse and they would approve or change my decision. It was so empowering to be able to have that kind of impact. Life changing, really." Rob finished his testimony, shaking his head at the memories.

"Thanks so much for sharing with us, Rob. Does anyone have questions for him?" Pastor Steve asked the group.

"How did you get involved with this missions team?" Scott asked.

"My parents' friend is a doctor, and he was

in charge of putting the teams together. I was there when he was talking to my mom and dad, so I asked if I could do it."

"Will you get to do it again, and how do you think it will affect your future?" Lindsay asked.

"Yes, I will do it every summer that I am able until I am old enough to make a permanent decision about where I feel God is leading me to serve. My future? My future will be in service to God. I can't say for sure that He will have me do this forever, but I would. Whatever He has for me is fine with me."

"You know," the minister interrupted, "this is a good time to share my brief message with you, and then we can go back to testimonies if anyone else has something to share. But Rob's testimony and devotion to serving God is so inspiring to me, and it brings me to a point. What is your life about? What is important to you? Really think about it. Yes, you are all in middle school and high school, and you're young. But who decides what too young is? Does God have age limits?"

He paused between each question to allow the students to consider them. "Rob did very grown-up things this summer in service to God and received untold blessings from the experience. What was your summer about? If you could define it in one word, what would you say the theme of your summer was?" Until that point, the questions hadn't needed an answer, but this time, the minister waited for someone to answer. "Let me rephrase my question. Tell me the one-word theme of your summer."

Lindsay paused for a moment, her heart pounding loudly in her chest, knowing exactly what her answer was. "Me. The one-word theme of my summer was *me*."

"Thank you for your honesty, Lindsay. Such is the truth with most of us. And it's never just our summers. Young people, correct me if I'm wrong." He looked around and made eye contact with the students in order to drive his point home. "The majority of your day, your life is spent focused on your pursuits—education, fun, experiences, material desires. Your basic needs and more are met for you. You don't have to think about where your next meal will come from. You don't have to wonder if you will be able to complete your education. You never wonder if you will receive medical treatment if you need it. With those things out of the way, you are left plenty of time to pursue the things that bring you pleasure. And you do it so well. We all do."

"Well. . . ," Scott interrupted with a perplexed look on his face.

"Yes, Scott, what are you thinking?"

"What are you saying? That we shouldn't be kids, we shouldn't be teenagers, and we shouldn't have the care that our parents give us? Are we wrong for going after an education and saving up for a car and stuff?"

"Well, some questions can only be answered between you and God, because I don't know your heart. But I'm certainly not saying that any of those things are absolutely wrong. But if they are propelled by an entitlement attitude—an attitude that suggests that you *deserve* all of those things—then yes, they become wrong because of that attitude.

The Bible tells us in James, chapter 1, that we should think of it as pure joy when we face hardships and trials because it proves that God is at work in our lives. A few verses later, we're told that it's the people who live humbly who should be proud of their high position and that it's the rich who should be aware of their lowly position. God doesn't have the same values we do. So if you are seeking His will, you'll be open to whatever He has for you, even if it's not always in line with what you think you want or deserve.

"As Christians, we can't walk through life unaware of the needs around us. We have to realize that, even when we have it so good, many people around us and around the world are suffering. Jesus came to reach those suffering people, and He asks us to partner with Him to do it. We can never be a part of that if our only focus is to drive our own agendas and get what we want all of the time. Our focus has to change from being about us and what we want, to being about Him and where He is working. With that corrected focus, it's a lot easier to live without certain privileges and pleasures, and it's also a lot easier to stay out of trouble. Do you think that if you have the singular focus of serving Jesus and allowing Him to serve others through you that you will make some of the dumb teenage choices you will be faced with? It's impossible."

"So," Steve posed a question, keeping the

dialogue flowing, "how do we do it? How do we change our focus and make our lives about everyone but ourselves? And once we know how to do it, we then have to answer the question of whether we want to. What do you think?"

The group remained quiet for a bit as the students considered Steve's words. It was clear that some of them were truly moved by Rob's testimony and Steve's message. Lindsay quietly contemplated her thoughts, and feeling the gentle tug that she had come to recognize as the leading of the Holy Spirit, she opened her mouth to speak but hesitated.

"What is it, Lindsay?" Steve asked. "Go ahead—be honest."

"Well, if I'm to be perfectly honest. . ." She hesitated again.

"It's okay to share openly. Go ahead, Linds," Steve prodded.

"Well, the thing is, I'm in eighth grade. I mean, am I not supposed to think of myself? Isn't that how growing up is supposed to be? But when I hear you talk and I consider Rob's words and what he did with his summer, I know in my heart that you're right, and I realize that Rob found another way. But part of me wishes that I hadn't heard this stuff. To be honest, it's a lot easier to be a kid and to let my parents take care of the details. Expectations from God are the last thing I thought I would have to face right now." Lindsay stopped talking even though she felt like she had more to say. She was conflicted.

"Thank you so much for your honesty," Steve encouraged her. "The reason that you feel so much conflict over this is that your spirit is at war with your flesh. That means that your heart, the part that the Holy Spirit leads, is fighting a battle with the human side of you, the side that Lindsay leads. Believe it or not, it's a good thing. We are told in Galatians, chapter 5, verse 17, 'For the sinful nature desires what is contrary to the Spirit, and the Spirit what is contrary to the sinful nature. They are in conflict with each other, so that you do not do what you want.' Jesus knows that we fight that battle with our humanity, and He encourages us to be victorious through Him. The problem is that it's not just a one-time victory and then it's settled. It's a daily struggle that we must fight. We have to surrender our wills and our desires to Him and choose each day to follow Him."

"Yes," Lindsay jumped in, "that battle you're talking about, that's exactly how I feel. But I know that I want to serve Jesus and I want to do what He asks me to, but I worry that sometimes I just won't be good enough."

Other students were listening intently, many of them feeling just as Lindsay did.

The youth minister got very quiet as he answered. "Lindsay, the thing is, you won't be good enough."

Everyone looked on in surprise. He had basically told her to give up and forget trying, right? She looked at him for a minute while she considered his words, and he waited before moving on. As soon as he saw the dawn of recognition in her eyes, he began to speak again.

"The beauty of being a Christian is that you will never be good enough. You will fail time and time again. If you could have been good enough, Lindsay, Rob, Sarah, Heather"—Steve looked around the campfire and called off each student's name—"if you had it in you to be good enough for even one day, then you would never have needed a Savior. But thankfully our Father

91

judges us through the blood of His Son, Jesus, if we have accepted Him as our personal Savior. We aren't judged by what we do; we are judged by what He did. Our actions are always and only a response to the grace we have been shown, never a way to earn that favor. Does that help? Does it maybe take some of the pressure off?"

Lindsay chuckled. "I don't know, maybe it adds pressure in some ways. . .but yes, I see what you're saying. Our acts of service or the choices we make aren't because we're afraid of God and some punishment we might receive; they are because we are in awe of His grace and living for Him in response to it."

"Yes, Lindsay, that's it exactly. I think with that said, we can close in prayer. Is there anyone here. . ."

Lindsay allowed Steve's closing words to trail off as she looked deeply into the fire and considered all that she had heard.

Chapter 8

I DARE YOU!

"I don't know if I'm going to Kelly's sleepover tonight, Mom." Lindsay hesitantly approached her mom about the upcoming event.

"What? Really? Why?" Her mom seemed confused because usually there was nothing more that Lindsay would rather do than hang out with her friends. Noticing Lindsay's discomfort, Mrs. Martin pressed for a bit more information. "Did you girls have a fight or something?"

"No, no, nothing like that," Lindsay assured her. "It's just that. . .well. . .I guess it's nothing." Not wanting to say something she'd regret, Lindsay tried to back out of the conversation. Her mom would have no part of that, though.

"Lindsay, what's going on? You need to be honest with me so I can help with whatever is troubling you."

"Mom, it's just that sometimes the girls sort of teeter on doing things or saying things that I'm not sure I'm comfortable with. Not bad, really, just enough to make me concerned about where it will all lead. I'm afraid of getting sucked into things that would cause problems." Lindsay squirmed. She felt a lot better after she expressed how she felt, even though it made her nervous. "Mom, I don't want you to think they're bad," she continued, "because they aren't."

"No, Lindsay, I know that they aren't bad. I also know that you are a very good and sensitive girl. It's a wonderful thing that you are concerned about this. Most people don't see trouble coming until it's too late. But recognizing that it's possible isn't enough. You have to decide for yourself what your choices will be when faced with temptation." Mrs. Martin paused to try to read Lindsay's expression.

When Lindsay nodded, her mom

continued. "It's not enough to know what right and wrong mean. You have to be strong enough to say no to temptation. Temptations will come throughout all of your life. There is no avoiding them. The problem isn't being tempted; it's what you do when you are. Instead of hiding from it and avoiding your friends, it's better to determine to do what is right and then to be an example of that to the people around you. Does that make sense?"

"Yes, Mom, you're totally right," Lindsay agreed. "It's just hard to be the odd one when your friends are having fun. Especially if it means you get teased."

"Yes, Linds, it is hard. That doesn't change, even as you get older. But just remember a time when Jesus was teased and taunted by the people He thought were His friends. He didn't waver or lose His focus, and He gave His life for those very people who were treating Him badly."

"All right, Mom, I'll go to the sleepover. I wouldn't really want to miss it, anyway. I just wasn't sure what to do."

"You'll be fine, Lindsay. I have faith in you." She reached across the couch and gave her daughter a hug. Lindsay silently hoped that she would be able to live up to her mom's faith in her.

"I'm here!" Lindsay shouted, coming through the gate in the wooden fence and letting it swing shut behind her.

Sam and Kelly were already in Kelly's swimming pool and were having a great time splashing and trying to push each other under the water. Before they even had a chance to respond, Lindsay was already taking off her T-shirt and shorts to uncover the swimsuit she was wearing underneath. She set her bag down, laid her clothes across the back of a chair, and took off for the diving board. She walked out to the end, bounced a few times, and then jumped straight in. After a few seconds, her head popped out of the water, and she sputtered until her face cleared. As soon as she opened her eyes, she was attacked with waves of water being splashed at her. Kelly and Sam were laughing hard as they attacked Lindsay. She fought back but to no avail. They pushed her under and then let her regain her footing.

Laughing and soaking wet, the three girls got out of the pool and went over to the cooler that Kelly had brought outside for them. Each girl took a soda just as they heard a car door slam in the driveway. Macy had arrived. She came smiling into the backyard, looking fantastic. Her diet had really begun to pay off, and she was picture-perfect in her cute little two-piece swimsuit. "Wow, girl!" Kelly whistled as Macy pushed her sunglasses to the top of her head. "You look great. Who are you trying to impress, though? Him?" Kelly pointed at her ten-year-old brother doing a cannonball off the diving board. They all ducked to avoid the splash and laughed at the suggestion.

"Ha, ha, right!" Macy laughed at the idea of trying to impress Kelly's little brother. "But you never know who you might see."

"I could invite Tyler over for you," Kelly suggested.

"Hey, speaking of him," Sam jumped in, "whatever happened after that phone call you made to his house last weekend?"

"Oh. . .I don't know. . . ," Macy coyly

responded with a twinkle in her eye.

"Come on. What haven't you told us?" Kelly demanded.

"Yeah, you'd better spill it," Lindsay agreed.

"Well, I don't really have anything to report—unless you'd call the movie we're going to go see Sunday afternoon a piece of information." Macy laughed at the shocked expressions of her friends.

"Are you kidding me?" Kelly shrieked.

"You're the first one of us to go on a date," Sam pointed out.

"Wow, I am soo impressed," Lindsay and Kelly said at the same time.

"How did you ever get your parents to agree to let you go?" Lindsay wondered.

"It's an afternoon movie, his mom is driving us and picking us up, and it's in a very public place. They really didn't put up too much of a struggle." Macy shrugged. "Believe me, I'm as surprised as you are."

"But the important question is, what are you going to wear?"

"Good question, Kelly. I was going to talk

to you about that later. I was hoping you'd let me raid your closet since most of my clothes are too big for me now and they aren't really date-type clothes."

"Oh definitely! We'll figure that out later tonight. For now, let's get to working on that tan of yours." Kelly's brother had gone inside, so the pool was calm and just waiting for them to come back in. They each grabbed a raft and climbed on top to sunbathe.

In Kelly's room, after they had their fill of sun and water, they decided to find an outfit for Macy to wear on her date. "Let's see," Kelly said, digging through her closet, "you have great legs, so let's go for a skirt or shorts."

"I think a skirt will look like I'm trying too hard, so let's try some shorts."

"Oh! What about these?" Kelly held up a pair of very short white denim shorts with a striped belt. "We'll find you a supercute top to go with them."

"There is *no way* those shorts are going to

fit me," Macy wailed.

"I'll bet they do fit. You've lost a ton of weight. Try them on," Sam encouraged.

Macy tried on the shorts, and they fit perfectly and showed off her toned and tanned legs beautifully. "Great. Now how about this top?" Kelly held up a hot pink halter top that matched the belt. Macy tried it on and couldn't believe how great she looked. When she came out of the bathroom with the outfit on, the other girls were absolutely speechless. No doubt about it, that was the outfit for her first date with Tyler—her first date ever.

A little while later, after they had eaten, it was time for their game. "Sam, you're first. Truth or Dare?" Macy asked Sam.

"I'll pick Dare," Sam said with a laugh. She was eager to get things going.

The three other girls left Sam on the floor while they conferred over Sam's dare. Scurrying back to the circle, the girls couldn't stop giggling about the dare they'd concocted.

Macy began. "Sam, your dare is to call Pizza Heaven—my brother is working delivery tonight—and order a pizza to be delivered to Stephanie Price's house." The girls giggled because Macy's brother, Zach, had liked Stephanie Price since the third grade. He could barely speak when she was nearby. "Use Stephanie's mom's name so that Zach won't figure out whose order it is until he's on his way to her house."

"Okay, that's easy," Sam replied.

"Wait," Lindsay said with concern. "Who is going to pay for the pizza?"

"That's their problem!" Kelly laughed.

"I don't know. . . ." Lindsay wasn't sure she liked that idea at all.

"Oh, don't be a party pooper." Kelly shrugged. "Besides, your turn is coming soon enough. I'd be more worried about that, if I were you." She finished with a laugh.

Sam had the phone book in her lap, and she'd already dialed the phone, so they all got very quiet and listened. "I'd like to order a pizza for delivery."

"I'd like a large thick-crust pizza, with pepperoni, onions, and anchovies."

At that, the girls found it difficult to control their laughter. Kelly had to leave the room for a second to compose herself while the other girls listened to Sam's end of the conversation.

"Actually, can you make that extra anchovies and extra cheese, too? . . . Please deliver it to 3654 Pennifield Lane. . . .Yes, that's right . . . . Do you take checks? . . . Thank you very much." She hung up the phone and rolled on the floor, trying to stop laughing, so she could tell the girls that the person on the phone had told her it would take just a little bit longer since they only had one delivery person that night. This was great news to the girls since it meant for sure that Zach would deliver the pizza.

Realizing that there was nothing they could do but wait to see if Zach ever tied the prank to them, they moved on with the game.

Macy's turn. "I'll take a Truth."

After a very short conference, the girls knew exactly what they wanted to ask Macy, so they returned to the circle.

"Macy, you must tell the truth. On your date with Tyler this Sunday, exactly what do you hope or imagine could happen? And you must provide *all* of the details that you have thought of, because we know you've imagined what could happen."

"Ugh, I knew it would be about this. Let's

see. . . . What do I think will happen?"

"No, not exactly. The question isn't about what you think will happen but what you hope *could* happen," Sam clarified.

"Well, first he'll come to the door and pick me up. My mom and dad will be there, and they'll want to talk to him. I would think his mom would be waiting in the car because she is going to drive us. My dad will probably lecture him on safety and on treating his daughter right, not that there is much that can happen at a movie. From there, we'll leave to head to the mall and his mom will drop us off. We'll go into the movie. I guess that's it."

"Oh no! No way are you getting off that easy. What have you imagined could happen during the movie?" Lindsay asked, getting into the spirit of it.

"Well, I'm sure we'll share a popcorn and maybe even a soda. I guess I hope that we share a soda rather than get our own. It seems more, um, personal that way, if you know what I mean." She paused for a reaction, and the girls nodded, encouraging her to continue. "So then we'll be sitting there, close to each other. Maybe we'll both put our arms up on the armrest at the same time and bump elbows. I'll leave my arm up there and hope he does the same so that our arms are touching."

The girls giggled in nervous embarrassment.

Macy hesitated, not wanting to continue.

"Come on," Kelly encouraged her. "Don't mind us; we're just jealous. Continue."

"The movie will continue for a little while, and we'll just stay that way, pretending not to notice. Then we'll reach into the popcorn at the same time. I might even wait until he reaches for it and make sure that I do, too. Our fingers will touch."

"Go on," Sam encouraged Macy.

"After that, I really hope he'll hold my hand for most of the rest of the movie. Then—" Macy stopped short, not wanting to finish her sentence, the part they all wanted to hear the most.

"Come on, Macy, you're doing great—don't quit now," Lindsay prodded.

"Yeah, you have to finish your truth," Sam reminded her.

"Well, this next part would probably never happen. This is a first date, and it's in public. But this is about my imagination, so I'll tell you how my daydream ends. We've been holding hands for a long time, and the movie is about to end, which means we'll have to leave the theater and meet up with Tyler's mom. So, he takes a deep breath, leans forward a little bit, and turns toward me. We share a soft, very tender kiss. The lights come on, and it's time to leave." Macy shrugged and pressed her hands to her burning cheeks. "There, that's it. That's the fantasy I have of my first date with Tyler Turner. Now go ahead and laugh."

"No way, we're not going to laugh. I hope it goes just the way you imagined, Macy," Sam said wistfully.

"Are you sure you want to kiss him already?" Lindsay asked, concerned. "Once you have your first kiss, you can't get it back. You want it to be special."

"Oh, it will be," Kelly assured them. "Macy's had a crush on Tyler Turner for so long that he should be her first kiss. No doubt about it."

"I just want her to be sure," Lindsay replied.

"Look at her; she's sure," Sam laughingly replied. Macy was sitting quietly, lost in her daydream, with a soft smile on her face as she imagined what it could be like.

"Kelly, Truth or Dare?" Lindsay asked.

"I'll pick Dare this time," Kelly answered confidently.

The girls conferred about Kelly's dare for quite a while. They were clearly in disagreement over what to choose. Kelly finally spoke up from across the room and said confidently, "Bring me whatever you've got, girls. I can take it." Sam and Macy jumped to their feet, eager to bring their dare to Kelly. Lindsay, with a shrug of her shoulders, reluctantly followed them back to the circle.

"Kelly, you have to drink a can of beer from the refrigerator upstairs—all of it," Sam challenged.

The three girls eyed Kelly expectantly. Surely this would be the dare that would break her and cause the first loss in the game of Truth or Dare.

"No problem!" Kelly jumped up confidently and headed up the stairs to the garage where her dad kept the beer in an old refrigerator. All three girls stared after her with openmouthed expressions. No one could believe that she was willing to do it.

Kelly came back into the kitchen from the garage and headed back downstairs to the basement where she took the can of beer out of the pocket on the front of her hooded sweatshirt. She winked at the girls and popped the can open and began to drink it. Although she tried to chug it down, it was too much for her, and she had to take several breaks. Eventually she was able to empty the can, and just for emphasis, she crushed it in her hand.

"I cannot believe that you just did that, Kelly." Lindsay said incredulously. She was shocked and shook her head in disbelief. She wanted to get into the spirit of things but simply could not believe what had just happened.

"How did it taste?" Macy wondered.

"You've never tasted beer?" Kelly asked.

"Nope," Macy replied.

"Me either," both Sam and Lindsay answered. "I tasted a sip of champagne at my cousin's wedding once," Sam added.

"Well, we'll have to change that sometime," Kelly teased, her words slurring a bit from the effects of the alcohol.

"Okay, Lindsay, your turn. And you have to pick Dare, remember?" Macy reminded her.

"Yeah, I know. Just be good to me, guys." Lindsay laughed nervously. She had prepared herself for this, and after seeing what Kelly agreed to do, she figured that her dare couldn't possibly be as difficult. She'd just do whatever it was and get it over with.

The girls huddled for just a moment and then returned to the circle to give Lindsay her dare.

"Lindsay, we dare you to go down to the store on the corner and buy a single can of beer," Kelly said confidently, sure that Lindsay wouldn't do it. "You don't even have to drink it," Kelly added.

"*What?*" Lindsay shouted. "I can't do that! For one thing, we're not allowed to leave the house. For another thing, my parents would have a fit if they knew I went to the store at this hour. And the last straw would be that I bought a can of beer. If I got caught, I would be in so much trouble. That would be the end of our sleepovers, that's for sure."

"Well, let me put it this way," Kelly said,

while the other girls sat silently waiting to see what would happen. "If you do it, you will prove that you not only keep your word, based on our deal when this game started, but you will also prove that you really are cool and fun to hang around with. And if you don't do it, you won't be able to be a part of the sleepovers or our group anymore."

Sam and Macy gasped in shock at Kelly's words. "Kelly, that's not what we. . ."

Kelly interrupted her. "Look, we said as a group that we were going to take this game very seriously. Consider it a test of her loyalty."

"But, Kelly, we don't want to put anyone's friendship on the line over a game," Macy pleaded with her.

"It's not just a game. It's a matter of honor. All four of us were there when these rules were decided, and we all agreed to uphold them. If she decides not to, then she has no honor and isn't interested in keeping her word to us."

Sam didn't even try to convince Kelly any longer and turned to Lindsay instead. "Linds, you're not going to get caught. You can just go right out the front door. The store is barely a block away—and if you try to buy the beer and they say no, you still did your part. Right, Kelly?"

"Oh yeah, if she tries but they say no, it's not her fault. We'll even walk with you and watch from outside the window."

Lindsay was about to cry. She didn't want to disappoint her friends, and she wanted to play along and be cool. But this was a big breach of trust, and it was just plain wrong. On the other hand, she would risk losing her best friends if she didn't do it. She didn't think there was anything that she wouldn't do for her friends. She loved her friends and couldn't imagine not having them in her life. But she also couldn't understand how they could sacrifice their friendship over a game. She was so torn over what to do—she felt that she couldn't win either way. But thinking of all their future plans together, she thought that she might lose a whole lot more if she didn't do it. She wished she had more time to decide. They were all staring at her, trying to figure out what she was going to do.

IT'S DECISION TIME!

The time has come to make a decision. Think long and hard about what you would really do if you encountered the circumstances Lindsay is facing. It's easy to say that you'd make the right choice. But are you sure that you could stand up to your friends and face their rejection? Once you make your decision, turn to the corresponding page to see how it turns out for Lindsay—and for you.

Turn to page 112 if you think that Lindsay is able to stand up to her friends by refusing to do the dare.

Turn to page 151 if Lindsay is unable to stand up to her friends and chooses to go ahead with the dare.

The next three chapters tell the story of what happened to Lindsay when she decided to do what she knew was right.

Chapter 9

DARING TO BE DIFFERENT

Lindsay's eyes welled up with tears. "I can't do this. I just can't. There's just no way that I would do something this risky that would get me into so much trouble with so many people. Plus, it's not how I operate. I just don't do things like that. I hope you all can just love me for who I am and not for whoever you're trying to make me."

The four girls sat quietly for a few minutes, while Lindsay wiped the tears from her eyes. They were at a sort of crossroads in their relationship. No one was happy that Lindsay decided not to perform the dare, but no one was surprised either. Lindsay picked at the rust-colored fibers of the old couch while she waited for someone to speak. Sam and Macy looked to Kelly and waited for her to take charge, as she usually did at such times.

"Well, first we have to see if someone else is willing to take on the dare. Who is next in the game?"

"It should probably start over with Sam," Macy answered, hoping to avoid the pressure of the dare falling to her.

"Okay, Sam, are you tough enough to take on the challenge of the dare that Lindsay isn't willing to perform?"

"Sure, Kelly, I'll do it for Lindsay," Sam offered, thinking that she was helping.

"Well, you won't actually be doing it *for* Lindsay—you'll be doing it *in place* of Lindsay, who, since she has decided that she is too good for us and our game, has given up her spot." Kelly spoke for the group, making up rules as she went along.

"My spot in the game or my spot in the group?" Lindsay asked hesitantly.

"They are one and the same," Kelly answered coldly, her judgment obviously impaired.

Sam and Macy gasped. This had gotten

way too serious. No one wanted to lose Lindsay's friendship, but they *had* made a deal, and Lindsay wasn't playing as an equal.

Lindsay was crying openly and tried to make another appeal for herself. "I don't understand why our friendship hinges on me doing something so completely wrong that puts me in danger of getting into lots of trouble. Why don't you all, as my friends, care about what I'm comfortable with and what I am afraid of? Do I mean so little to you that a stupid challenge is enough to erase all of these years of loyalty and friendship?"

"You're proving your loyalty. Your loyalty is to your stupid rules and your dumb church. I always wondered if they were more important to you than we are, but now I know for sure. "

"No, you're missing the point. I'm not choosing my church and my rules—as you call them, which, by the way, aren't nearly as stupid as the rules you've made up for this game—over you guys. I'm choosing right over wrong, doing the right thing over doing the dare. But if you can't see that, I guess we aren't really the friends I thought we were anyway. How about you, Sam and Macy?" Lindsay asked, wanting to find out exactly where she stood. "Are you in agreement with this?"

At the same moment, both Sam and Macy silently looked away, telling Lindsay just how they felt about it.

"Well, I'm going to call my mom to come and get me, and then you three can continue your fun." Lindsay went to the phone and called home, asking her mom to come and pick her up. She didn't tell her much of the story over the phone, but Mrs. Martin could tell from the sound of her daughter's voice that this was very different than a five-year-old calling home because she missed her mommy.

"I'll be right there, Linds."

Lindsay gathered up her belongings: her swimsuit that was still drying over the shower curtain in the basement bathroom, the toothbrush she had left on the vanity, the snacks she had brought to share. . .and she also grabbed a few items that she had left there during past visits. She placed all the items into her backpack and silently walked to the front porch, where she sat on the stoop crying softly while she waited for her mom to arrive.

At just after one in the morning, Mrs. Martin pulled into the driveway, and Lindsay rose from the stoop, collected her things, and, with her head down, made the lonely walk to the car. Mercifully her mom didn't say anything on the short drive home because Lindsay was withdrawn, quiet, and not quite ready to talk about what had happened.

When they arrived home, Mrs. Martin helped Lindsay get her things out of the car and set them on the tile floor in the foyer just inside the front door. Thinking that Lindsay might need some company and might be ready to talk, she went into the kitchen and put some water into the teakettle to heat for hot chocolate.

Lindsay went to wash up in the bathroom and then walked back down the hallway to join her mom. She was hesitant, because she didn't know quite what to say or how much to tell her mom. When she entered the kitchen and her mom looked up at her from the kitchen table, Lindsay started to cry.

"Oh, sweetie." Mrs. Martin was instantly on her feet and held her daughter as she cried big, sad tears. "Do you want to talk about it?"

"Mom, they—they—they picked a game over me. They didn't have any respect for what I wanted. They don't even know m—m—me, really." Lindsay was crying and not making much sense.

"Slow down, honey. Let's take this one step at a time. Tell me what happened—from the beginning."

"Well, we were playing a game. It started back a few weeks ago when we first started our Friday night sleepovers. The game was a sort of deal that we made. It's called Truth or Dare." Lindsay noticed the look of recognition on her mom's face. "You've heard of it?"

"Linds, everyone has played Truth or Dare. It's not anything new."

"Well, we played seriously. It was a matter of honor to take your turn and either answer the question truthfully or perform your dare with no complaints." Lindsay paused to take a deep breath and blow her nose. "Well, it was my turn, and I picked Dare because they were all mad that I was only choosing Truth." Lindsay started to rush her story, wanting to get it all out as quickly as possible. "My dare was horrible, and I couldn't do it, and they said that if I didn't do it, I was out of the group. But I didn't do it, and so they told me I had to leave, so I called you."

"Okay, slow down. Take a deep breath. What was the dare?"

"I can't tell you yet, Mom."

"Why not? Oh, you mean they still might be doing whatever it is they dared you to do?"

Lindsay nodded, her eyes downcast.

"Lindsay," Mrs. Martin said sternly, "if your friends are in any danger or if they are doing something to endanger someone else, you need to tell me."

"They aren't my friends, and I don't think they're in danger. I'll tell you what they're doing, though," Lindsay pulled a chair out from the table and slumped into it. "I was given a dare, and since I wouldn't do it, they made me leave. But Sam had to take on my dare in my place. She has to leave the house with the other girls following and walk down to the corner store and buy a can of beer. She doesn't have to drink it or anything, just buy it."

Mrs. Martin looked horrified. "Lindsay,

first of all, I am very proud of you for having no part in that dare. We'll talk more about that later, though. For now, we have a big problem. Are you aware that not only will they be in trouble with their parents but also with the police? Buying alcohol as a minor is illegal. If they attempt to do it, the shop owner will have to call the police, and they will likely be arrested."

"I thought it was illegal only if we drank it!" Suddenly Lindsay was scared for her friends and worried that something horrible was about to happen.

Lindsay noticed that Mrs. Martin was dialing the phone. "Mom!"

She held her hand up to Lindsay and began to tell the story to Kelly's mom.

Finishing up her conversation, Mrs. Martin said, "Well, I just got home. So, since I'm still dressed, I'll head over there right now and see if I can stop this from happening." She hung up the phone and grabbed her purse, cell phone, and keys and headed for the door. As a last thought, she stopped and scribbled a note to Lindsay's dad in case he woke up before they got back. She hurried to the garage, Lindsay scrambling along after her—there was no way she was going to stay home.

They made the short drive back toward Kelly's house and turned the corner to drive to the convenience store. As soon as they made the turn toward the store, they could see the lights. There were two police cars in the parking lot with their lights flashing on top. "Oh no! We're too late!" Lindsay cried.

"Lindsay, it's not your fault that this happened. And maybe getting caught is the best thing that could happen to the girls. They will hopefully learn a lot from this experience. Let's go see what we can do, though." Mrs. Martin parked her car and got out, motioning for Lindsay to stay in her seat. Lindsay didn't argue, because she wasn't in any hurry to see her presumably angry friends, anyway.

From the car, Lindsay could see into the store through the big plate glass front window. She saw her three friends, with their backs against the checkout counter, facing the policeman who stood in front of them, obviously questioning the girls. Lindsay felt so bad for her friends. They didn't know that what they were trying to do was illegal—they did know it was wrong, though.

The three girls turned to face the counters,

and the policewoman who had been quiet stepped forward and spoke sternly to the crying girls. Mrs. Martin approached them and tried to reason with the police but was motioned to step back and stay out of the situation. Because she wasn't one of the girls' mothers and she didn't have a child involved in the prank, there was nothing she could do but use her cell phone to call their parents.

Since Kelly's mom was already on her way, Mrs. Martin dialed Sam's home first. Sam was in the most trouble because she was the one who had actually asked for the beer. Mrs. Martin cried as she told Mrs. Lowell the story. There was nothing left to say, so she hung up the phone and called Macy's house.

Lindsay sat in the car, quietly praying for her ex-friends, worried about the trouble that they had gotten into and what would happen to them—and to their friendship.

Back in the Martins' cheery kitchen, Lindsay felt anything but cheerful as she sipped her reheated hot chocolate. She impatiently waited for her mom to finish her phone conversation so she could find out what had happened to her friends.

"Lindsay," her mom started hesitantly after she hung up the phone, "that was Kelly's dad; her mom was too upset to answer her cell phone. It seems that they are going to make examples of the girls. Sam is in trouble for attempting to purchase alcohol, and Kelly is in even bigger trouble for consuming alcohol. They discovered that she drank an entire can of beer. I thought you said that there was no drinking involved?"

Lindsay buried her head in her hands and sobbed. She was so sad and scared for her friends but also relieved that she had avoided, though narrowly, this trouble for herself. Between her tears, she attempted to answer her mom. "There was no drinking involved in my dare, but Kelly's dare was to drink an entire can of beer from her parents' refrigerator. I should have stood up to them then. Maybe this whole thing could have been avoided." She continued to cry, shaking her head.

"Sweetie, there are a lot of things about tonight that I wish had gone differently. But one thing I am confident of is that I am so proud of you for taking the stand you did. Whether it should have been sooner or could have been done differently isn't the question. Each one of you girls is responsible for—and will have to pay for—your own actions. In your case, you've only made me more proud of you and more confident in your trustworthiness. You faced some very difficult and very adult decisions tonight, Lindsay, and you did the right things even though they were very hard. In fact, it's because your choices were so hard that they are so honorable.

"I know it seems pretty bleak right now. Not only do you feel like you lost your best friends, but you still love them and know that they are suffering right now." Lindsay was crying so hard that her shoulders were shaking. "Lindsay, honey, it's going to be okay."

"I know, Mom, I'm just so. . .relieved. And I feel guilty about that. But I am so glad that I did what I did."

"I have an idea. Let's pray for the girls right now," Mrs. Martin suggested.

"Okay, Mom."

"Father in heaven, thank You for keeping all four of these girls safe tonight. Thank You for giving Lindsay the strength and confidence she needed to withstand the pressures that she endured from the other girls. Please protect those three girls and help them to learn a valuable lesson from all of this, and please help Lindsay to continue to be used as a witness for You in the midst of this tragedy. Amen."

"Amen."

Chapter 10

OUT OF THE CLUB

The walk into the school was a very lonely one for Lindsay. She kept her head down and put one foot in front of the other until she found herself at her locker. She didn't want to see if her friends were talking near their favorite tree—and she especially didn't want to see if they weren't. Kelly and Sam weren't taking calls from Lindsay, and Macy wasn't allowed to come to the phone, so Lindsay didn't have any new word on what had happened on Friday night.

Without looking around at the students milling in the halls, she slowly gathered the things she would need from her locker for her first class. She wasn't in any hurry to get to class, so she stood there for much longer than she actually needed to.

"Hey, can I talk to you for a minute?" a male voice said from right behind her left ear.

Lindsay jumped with a startled squeal and turned to face Tyler Turner, who stood at her locker with a sad look on his face. He wore his typical outfit: baggy jeans and a baseball T-shirt with a ball cap on his head. But today, somehow he just looked dark. His black jeans and dark gray T-shirt along with the black baseball cap seemed to match the expression on his face: dark and sad.

"Yeah, sure, what's up?" Lindsay was pretty sure she already knew what he wanted to talk to her about.

"Um, well, Macy and I were supposed to have a movie date yesterday, but she didn't answer her phone, didn't answer her doorbell, and never called to tell me what happened. It's almost as if she just completely blew me off. Did I do something to upset her?" Tyler looked perplexed and genuinely concerned.

"You mean you haven't heard what happened?" Lindsay asked with disbelief.

"No, I haven't heard anything." Tyler seemed to realize all of a sudden that something could actually have gone wrong. "Is Macy hurt? Is she okay?" he asked frantically.

"Yes, Macy is fine. She's in quite a bit of trouble and was probably not allowed to use the phone. I'm going to be late to class, and I don't really want to talk about it. Just know that she'll be okay, and she'll fill you in on the details when she's ready. And, um, her part in the trouble isn't as bad as it could have been, if that helps at all." She turned immediately to leave, hoping to escape without any more questions.

"Wait, I just need to know one more thing," Tyler begged, needing reassurance. "Before this thing happened, was she excited about our date?"

"Yes, Tyler, she was very excited. I promise you that." At that moment, the bell rang and the two parted ways without saying another word.

The first class of the day wasn't too bad, but by second period, word had started to get around and kids were looking at Lindsay with funny expressions. She could feel their stares as she walked down the hall. She was sure that some of them would make fun of her for leaving the girls' party. But at that point, she didn't care.

The worst moment came when she had to enter home ec. Knowing that it was the final week to work on their project in class, Lindsay was dreading what was sure to be a very awkward and uncomfortable hour. But they had to complete their project so it could be presented to the class the next week.

Standing outside the classroom, waiting until the last second before the bell rang to slip in, hoping to avoid the awkward silence before class started, Lindsay said a quick prayer. Just as the bell was about to ring, she walked in with her head held high. She noticed that none of her friends were in their seats. She hadn't seen them all day, but she had thought that they must be avoiding her, not that they were absent. She became very worried and approached her teacher. "Mrs. Portney, I don't think any of my group members are here. Are they sick or something?"

"Well, Lindsay, I don't think it's that they're sick. I am sure you're aware of some of the circumstances from the weekend." When Lindsay nodded silently, Mrs. Portney continued.

"They are on a school suspension for a short time until the administration decides what needs to be done."

"Oh, I see." Lindsay slumped back to her seat and sat at their big table all by herself. She quietly spread the craft items in front of her after deciding to go ahead and finish the project on her own. She got lost in her work until the bell rang, and without a word to anyone else, she packed up and left for lunch, where she also sat alone. It was becoming too much to bear. The loneliness. The worry. The fear. The embarrassment. She felt her eyes welling up with tears, so she escaped to the hallway where she could use the phone to call her mom.

"Mom, it's horrible!" Lindsay cried into the phone. "The kids are all staring at me, and Sam, Macy, and Kelly aren't even in school today. They're suspended. What's happening to them?"

"Slow down, sweetie. I know you only have a few minutes, so just listen to me. The girls are fine. I've spoken to Mrs. Lowell and Mrs. Monroe. Yes, they are suspended for three days, but they'll be back in school on Thursday. And yes, they are in trouble at home, of course, and will have a punishment to deal with for quite a while, I would imagine. We aren't sure yet what the legal situation will be, but these are young girls who have never been in trouble before. Whatever happens, they can and will get through it. The important thing for you to remember, Linds," Mrs. Martin stressed, "is that you did the right thing. Let things play out now, and they will work out. Everything has a way of working out. Be resolved to use this to build your reputation. Don't slink away because of it. Use it as part of your witness for Jesus, or it will be all for nothing. Just hold your head up high, and show your confidence."

"Okay, Mom. That really helps. I'm going to do it. At least now I don't have to worry so much about what's happening to the girls. I have to go now—the bell's about to ring."

"Bye, Lindsay. I love you."

"I love you, too, Mom."

The week crept by while Lindsay waited for her friends to come back to school. On one hand, she couldn't wait to see them, to see if they were really okay; but on the other hand, she dreaded facing the fact that they really wanted nothing to do with her. One thing she knew for sure: She was really looking forward to being out of the limelight and past the whispering stage. The other kids were so curious about what had happened that they either came right out and asked Lindsay every chance they got, or worse, they whispered behind her back and speculated about what might have happened.

The most difficult part of the week was continuing with the pillow the group had been making for home ec class. It was supposed to be a group project, but Lindsay had to finish it by herself. She asked Mrs. Portney if there was anything else she could do, but her teacher urged her to continue and use the class time wisely. So the pillow was almost complete. Lindsay was hoping that on Thursday the other girls would be able to put some personal finishing touches on it—if they would even speak to her.

On Wednesday afternoon, Lindsay went home right after school, as had been the pattern all week long. She sat in the family's formal dining room to complete her homework. Distracted by the birds being chased by a squirrel in the backyard, Lindsay stared out the large, plate glass bay window.

As her thoughts wandered, she didn't hear the sound of a car pulling into their long driveway, nor did she hear the doorbell ring. Moments later, Mrs. Martin escorted a very timid Macy into the dining room. "Sweetie, someone is here to see you. I'll leave you two to talk, and Mrs. Monroe and I will be in the kitchen having a cup of coffee."

Lindsay was silent as she looked at her friend. She willed herself not to cry but was quickly losing the battle. The tears started to form, and knowing there was nothing she could do about it, she let them fall.

Macy ran to her side and hugged her. "Lindsay, I am so sorry. Can you ever forgive me?" Macy begged.

"Of course I can, and I do. I missed you. I miss all of you."

"I know, Linds. I just can't believe that things turned out like they did. Kelly and Sam got into so much trouble. I am just in trouble at home, not with the police—but it's bad enough.

My mom is here because she knew I needed to talk to you, but she's only giving me a few minutes. She is disappointed in me for the way I treated you. I'm just so sorry, Lindsay."

"Look, Mace, remember that talk the school counselor gave last year about peer pressure and how it's easy to get caught in the moment? It's that way with Sam and Kelly. They have a way of persuading us to do stuff, knowing we'll go along with them just because we want to make everyone happy. I'm not saying that makes it okay, just that's the way it is. Since this happened, my mom and I have talked a lot about how the decisions we make now—and how we learn from them—will help shape who we will become as we grow up. Give yourself a break. We all make mistakes, but we need to learn something and try not to make them again. It doesn't mean the world is coming to an end. It also doesn't mean I don't want to be your friend."

"But—but," Macy stuttered as she fought through her own tears, "I let them make fun of you—I let them kick you out of the group. How can you forgive me so easily?"

"Oh, Macy, no one's perfect. It's like my

youth pastor is always saying: We're all imperfect, all sinners, but God freely offers forgiveness to us through the sacrifice of His own Son. If Jesus gave Himself to die so I could be forgiven for my sins, how can I not forgive you? The Bible says that once God forgives us, He forgets about our sins. So what do you say we just forget about this?"

"Oh, Lindsay, I'm so glad to hear you say that, and you're so right. But I can't forget about this. It's going to be going on for a long time, just eating at me."

"Well, I wasn't meaning that we should forget about the consequences," Lindsay explained. "They have to be faced. But our friendship can be healed. We can put that part of it behind us right now."

"I'd really love that, Lindsay."

"Done." The girls laughed together and both breathed a deep sigh of relief.

"Just remember what I told you about God's forgiveness. It's a free offer. You know that."

"I know, and I think I'm starting to understand how that works."

Macy's mom came into the room and told

her that it was time to go. Macy and Lindsay would see each other at school the next morning. Macy asked Lindsay if she would be waiting by the tree.

"Um, no," Lindsay answered. "There are other things that have to be taken care of before that can happen. I'll just be in the school getting ready for class. I'll see you in home ec, though."

As Macy and her mom were getting ready to leave, Mrs. Monroe paused with her hand on the brass doorknob. "Lindsay, I just wanted to tell you that I am very proud of you, and I am grateful for your influence in Macy's life. I heard a lot of what you said in the dining room, and, well, I'm just very proud of you."

They left without waiting for a reply, and Lindsay quietly shut the door behind them. She turned to find her mom standing there, watching her, softly smiling. Lindsay took a step toward her and was immediately engulfed in motherly, comforting arms. Healing had begun.

Thursday morning came too quickly for Lindsay.

She dreaded the walk into the school and the effort it would take to avoid Kelly and Sam. It would also be difficult to see Macy with Sam and Kelly, but she had to let Macy find her own way through the confusion.

She dressed carefully—not wanting to appear too eager but also not wanting to look like she didn't care. She chose to wear the same outfit that she wore to school on the first day, hoping that since they helped her pick it out, it might make the other girls feel nostalgic for a time when things were much less complicated.

With her backpack slung casually over one shoulder and her head held high, Lindsay walked into the school a full ten minutes before the time that she usually met the girls under the tree in the school yard. She got what she needed from her locker and then slipped into her first-period classroom, choosing a desk near the window where she could look out onto the yard unnoticed.

The school bus pulled up to the curb, and students began to file off with their piles of books and backpacks. The last three to exit the bus were Macy, Sam, and Kelly who, for some reason, all rode the bus that day. They were laughing and looking as though they hadn't a care in the world. They sauntered over to their tree and casually leaned against it while they talked and laughed. Lindsay looked on from her desk at the window, amazed that they seemed so carefree. Then she noticed that Sam and Kelly were both wearing dark sunglasses and Kelly had a hat on her head. They were hiding in their own way, while trying to look at ease.

At that moment, Kelly turned and noticed Lindsay watching from the window. She nudged Sam and pointed at the school, whispering something to her. They both stared at Lindsay for a moment and held her gaze before they looked away in disgust. Lindsay was heartbroken but could not tear her eyes away from the scene. The three girls started to walk into the school, Macy last. She looked at Lindsay with pity and longing, wishing that things could be very different—but they weren't. They had created this situation; now they had to face it.

Chapter 11

MAKING AMENDS

Well before class was to start, Lindsay walked into the home economics room and asked Mrs. Portney if there was something else she could do during the class period to give Macy, Sam, and Kelly a chance to work on their project alone since they had missed so many days. In truth, Lindsay wanted to avoid having to work with them and thought that just missing the class entirely was a good option. Mrs. Portney understood that there was a problem going on, so she wisely said that it just wasn't an option. She asked Lindsay to stay in class and face up to her challenges. She recommended that Lindsay just be bigger than the problem, act maturely and confidently, and show that she was not bothered by any of it.

As Lindsay was leaving the room to visit her locker before the bell rang, resigned to do as her teacher asked, Mrs. Portney stopped her so that she could make one last comment. "Lindsay, I just wanted to tell you that I think I've heard enough of the story of what went on last weekend to confidently say that I'm very proud of you for your strength of character and your willingness to defend your principles. You did the right thing, and everything will work out better than you could even imagine. Now go ahead, and get your things."

Lindsay nodded and ducked out of the classroom. She gathered the few books she needed for her afternoon classes and headed back to the home ec room. As she arrived, she saw that Kelly, Sam, and Macy were entering the classroom just ahead of her. She took a deep breath, straightened her shoulders, held her head up high, and confidently walked into the classroom. She walked to her seat and calmly sat next to her friends. Macy quietly caught her gaze from across the table and gave her a slight wink, just enough to boost Lindsay's confidence and convince her that she was doing well.

"Settle down, class. Let's quiet down and pay attention." Mrs. Portney waited until the class had settled down and stopped talking before continuing. "This is the very last class period that you have to work on your projects, so please use the time wisely. Tomorrow will be the day for you to present your projects to the class and share your findings and cost comparisons. Now, get to work."

"I set it up with Mrs. Portney just before class," Kelly immediately jumped in, avoiding all small talk. "We can take our things to the library and work on our pillow there so that we can keep it a surprise from the class." The four of them gathered their things and quietly left the classroom. No one knew quite what to say. Lindsay broke the ice.

"I don't want this to be uncomfortable. If you guys want, since I did a lot of work on the pillow while you were out of school, I can just read or something while you three finish up the pillow."

"No way!" Macy would have none of that. "We started this together—we'll finish it together."

Sam and Kelly had looked like they had been about to go along with Lindsay's plan, but when Macy made her statement, they reluctantly agreed. "Besides, it could affect your grade if you don't participate, Lindsay," Macy continued.

To that, Kelly rolled her eyes. "Not like she'd risk getting into trouble."

Lindsay took a deep breath. "I just have to say this, and then we can do our work." Lindsay had had enough and wanted to get her feelings off her chest. "Kelly, you're selfish. You want things just how you want them, and if anyone goes against you, you have no use for her. I am a person, too. I have plans, feelings, emotions, limits, likes, and dislikes, just like you do. I also have the capability to make a decision about what I want for myself. If you ever hope to have a real friend and not just a follower, then you'll have to learn to appreciate the differences in people and give others room to be themselves. Otherwise, rather than real friends, you'll always only have people around you until they are tired of just following your orders and taking your bullying."

Kelly stared at her with her mouth open. No one had ever spoken up to her that way. Sam spoke up. "Hold on, Lindsay, I take offense to that. Are you saying that I am just a follower and can't make up my own mind?"

"Well, think about it, Sam. That whole night, all of the dares—they were Kelly's idea. When I refused, it was Kelly who demanded that I be cut out. You and Macy didn't want to, but you went right along with Kelly. Macy at least had the guts to come to me and apologize."

Kelly glared at Macy when she heard that.

"See?" Lindsay whispered emphatically. "It makes you crazy mad, Kelly, to think that Macy came and apologized to me, that she would want to be my friend even though you said she couldn't."

Macy tentatively opened her mouth. "You know what? I agree with Lindsay completely. I don't want to be a follower. I want to be my own person. My heart tells me that Lindsay is one of my best friends, and I'm not willing to turn my back on her just to follow the orders of another one of my best friends. I think that you need to do some soul-searching, Kelly, and decide what you want out of your friendships and if you're willing and able to respect us as people and appreciate our differences rather than try to erase them."

Sam had been quiet for a while, but it seemed like some of the things she was hearing had gotten to her. She quietly said, "I'm sorry, Lindsay; you're totally right. I'm sorry for how I've been acting. Can you forgive me?"

"Of course I can, and I do. It's over and done."

"Well, if you three are finished, we have some work to do." Kelly was having no part of the apologies and wanted to change the subject.

Lindsay showed them what she had done to their pillow while they were out of school. There wasn't a whole lot of work that remained, so Kelly, Sam, and Macy set about to complete the pillow while Lindsay worked on finalizing the cost and material comparison report. The four girls finished their work at about the same time, and they sat back to survey the results.

All four of them laughed when they

stepped back to really look at their finished pillow. It looked just like Mrs. Portney. To prove it, Sam took the pillow up to the circulation desk and asked the librarian, Mrs. Woods, to look at the pillow and see if it reminded her of anyone.

Mrs. Woods looked up from the book she was reading and lowered her glasses so she could peer over the top of them at the pillow in Sam's hands. Immediately she started to laugh. "Well, I'll be. It's a Portney Pillow." She laughed until she had to wipe the tears from her eyes. After she composed herself, she said, "You girls have done a great job on that pillow. It looks just like her down to the littlest details. Great job."

Confidently the four girls headed back to class to get everything put away before the bell rang. Their Portney Pillow was carefully wrapped in plastic and stowed in their bin, awaiting the day they could reveal it. They gathered their things and readied themselves to head off to their next class. Lindsay, trying not to be too intrusive, moved to leave immediately so that the others could walk together.

Kelly reached out and grabbed her backpack and softly tugged her back. "Linds, just give me some time to figure things out. I heard everything that you said, and I'm not a completely coldhearted person. I just need some time. But you don't need to leave. You didn't do anything wrong. I just have to figure out what I did wrong." With that, Kelly left alone, leaving Sam, Macy, and Lindsay to stare after her, dumbfounded.

"Wow, I guess miracles can happen," Macy said.

"Pray, girls. Just pray," Lindsay encouraged them.

As Lindsay woke up Friday morning, she thought she heard the phone ringing, but it was hazy. A few moments later, there was a knock at her door and her mom was standing there holding the cordless phone. "Lindsay, it's Macy on the phone for you."

Lindsay groggily sat up in her bed and reached for the phone while rubbing her eyes as they adjusted to the bright sunshine streaming through the windows. "Hello? Macy?"

"Hey, Linds, I just wanted to catch you before you left for school. I know that you've been trying to get there early so you can go hide out in your classroom." She hesitated as she chose her next words carefully. "I just. . . I guess I just don't think that's fair. Sam and I want you to come to our tree. There's nothing that you should be hiding from. You didn't do anything wrong."

"Macy, I really appreciate that you're concerned about this, but I really don't want to cause any more problems. I really want to give Kelly the time that she asked for and see what happens without pushing it."

"I know, Lindsay, and I can respect that, but I also think that if we don't all show Kelly that we aren't going to accept things as they are, it won't make her sit up and take notice. She needs to realize that it's not her call. She can take the time she needs, and we're all there for her, but she can't control us in the process."

"Okay, here's what I'm going to do, Mace," Lindsay explained. "Since I'm up so early and now have plenty of time before school"—both girls laughed—"I'm going to talk about it with my mom and pray about it. I just want to do the right thing and not mess up any progress that we've already made."

"Lindsay, I think that's a great idea," Macy agreed. "You know, I think you're the wisest person I know."

"Thanks, Mace. I'll see you at school one way or another."

Lindsay decided that she needed to approach Kelly alone so that she didn't feel bombarded by all of them at once. So she went to another tree and waited there. The tree in Kelly's front yard seemed to be the perfect place. Kelly would see her standing there when she came out to walk the dog before she and her mom left for school. So Lindsay waited.

After about five minutes, the front door opened and Kelly appeared in the entrance, struggling with their golden retriever, Abby. She started to walk out to the front yard but stopped short when she saw Lindsay waiting there. "Hey," Kelly said without emotion. She was trying to pretend that she wasn't interested in talking to Lindsay.

"Hey, Kell. I thought it was time that we talked. Don't you think this has gone on long enough?"

"Yeah, I guess so. Where do we go from here, though? I mean, how can we possibly fix this?"

"Well, the way I see it, I've already told you the ways I feel I've been hurt. Now you can respond to that if you want to. And if I have done anything to hurt you, this would be the time for you to tell me."

"See, that's the thing, Lindsay. You're perfect. You haven't done anything wrong, and you never will. I can never measure up to you. You'll always be strong enough to be your own person."

"What is it about that that scares you? Is it because you can't control me? So what? It's not a competition. I love you for who you are, and I don't want to change you. Why do you want to change me?"

Kelly began to cry. "I know that's how you feel, but it's easy for you. You have nothing to worry about. You don't care if people like you or not—but they always do, because you're perfect.

It's different for me. Before you girls, I didn't really have best friends. I guess I was afraid—afraid that when you said you liked Macy best of all of us, it meant the two of you might go off and just be friends without me and that Sam would go with you because she likes you better. I thought if I kicked you out, they'd stop liking you."

"But, Kelly, don't you see, maybe that's the reason you feel like you never had friends before us. I love you for who you are, and yet you still pushed me away instead of just letting us love you and trusting that we can each do our own thing and still stay friends."

"You're right, Lindsay; you're totally right. I'm so sorry. Can you ever forgive me?"

"It's already done, Kelly. And someday, maybe I'll be able to tell you about real forgiveness. For now, we need to get to school and put this behind us. Deal?"

They hugged in Kelly's front yard, and Lindsay just held Kelly while she sobbed some cleansing tears that celebrated the freedom in forgiveness.

The next three chapters tell the story of what happened to Lindsay when she decided to give in to peer pressure by going through with the dare.

Chapter 9

I'LL DO IT!

The minutes seemed like a lifetime as Macy and Sam waited for Lindsay to decide. Kelly, feigning disinterest, picked at her fingernails while she waited. She looked up after a minute or two and said, "Well, this isn't that difficult of a decision. You're either in, or you're out. What's it going to be?"

"I can't believe I'm saying this, but I'll do it. Let's just go and get it over with—fast!" Lindsay got up immediately, and her surprised friends followed her up the stairs. She hurriedly slipped on her sandals and quietly opened the front door, hoping it wouldn't squeak. One by one, each girl slipped through the open door, and then, making sure it wasn't locked, Lindsay carefully and silently closed it.

They giggled as they walked down the sidewalk toward the convenience store—everyone but Lindsay. She was so nervous that she spent the entire walk fighting off tears.

"Hey, Lindsay," Kelly said, "you've got to pull it together. If you go in there looking like that, you'll never be allowed to buy the beer. You need to look confident and carefree—not like you're facing a firing squad."

"You're right," Lindsay said, laughing. "I can do this. It'll be fine. I won't get caught. It's almost over. . . ." She recited encouragement to herself, hoping it would boost her confidence.

They arrived at the store much too soon for Lindsay's comfort, but she did just want to get her task over with and then get back safely to the comfort of Kelly's house as fast as possible.

The three girls walked over to the large windows where they could peer between the advertisements and signs to watch Lindsay as she carried out her dare. Lindsay walked up to the door, took a deep breath, squared her shoulders, and opened the door. It swung toward her with the jingling of bells that hung from the top of the door to alert the shopkeeper that a customer was entering the store. He was behind the counter reading a newspaper and looked up for only a second to notice Lindsay. Apparently she didn't look like much of a threat because he went back to reading his paper.

Lindsay considered heading straight for the refrigerator cases at the back and getting it over with but decided that she would be more believable if she shopped for a few other items first. So she wandered down the aisles and selected a loaf of bread, a pack of gum, a bottle of water, and then went to get her can of beer. She opened the door to the cooler where the single cans were stored, and without checking the price or brand, she just grabbed the closest one to her and let the door swing shut. It bounced off the frame with a bang that startled both Lindsay and the shopkeeper, who put his newspaper down to keep an eye on her.

Remembering that it didn't matter if the clerk allowed her to buy it or not, Lindsay figured that it was safe to make her purchases.

She stood up very straight as she walked to the cash register, hoping that she looked much older than her age. As she approached the clerk, she had a great idea—so she thought. She would tell the cashier that the beer was for her dad. That way he wouldn't be so hesitant to sell it to her. After she placed her items on the counter, she took out her wallet.

Without even looking at the items he was scanning, the clerk put them into the bag one at a time. Lindsay hoped that he wouldn't even notice the beer. He picked up the cold can to scan it but looked down first. With a small gasp, he looked from the can of beer to Lindsay and then back to the beer. He opened his mouth to speak, but Lindsay interrupted, "Oh, don't worry, it's for my dad. He sent me down here to pick that up for him." The clerk looked at her for a moment, clearly not sure what he should do.

"Okay, give me just one second. I'm out of the right kind of bags up here. A paper bag won't work for a cold can. It will just break right through." He hustled toward the back room.

Lindsay was so relieved. It looked like everything was going smoothly, so she turned to

154

give the girls a thumbs-up. They were still staring through the window, and Kelly was smiling smugly. She was clearly surprised and pleased that Lindsay had carried out her dare.

The shopkeeper slowly walked from the back room with his arms full of bags. Once back at the cash register, he began to stock the bags of all sizes into their respective bins. "Sorry, I just figured that since I was back there, I'd grab some of each size."

"Oh, it's all right," Lindsay said, clearly relaxing. "I'm not in any hurry."

At that very moment, Lindsay noticed a lot of activity at the front window and turned to see what was happening. A police car pulled into the parking lot with its lights flashing and the siren off. Two policemen exited the car; one went over to where Sam, Kelly, and Macy were standing, and the other one headed for the front door of the store.

"What's going on?" Lindsay asked the shopkeeper in a panic.

"You kids need to be taught a lesson," he sputtered back at her.

Both policemen had entered the store and

were eyeing Lindsay as they asked the clerk what the trouble was. He told them that she had been attempting to purchase alcohol. He had called because he was tired of kids trying to get away with this and knew that he could get into a lot of trouble if he sold it to her.

"You did the absolute right thing by calling us," one of the policemen assured him. "So, miss, what is your name, and how old are you?"

"M–m–my name is Lindsay," she stammered. "I'm thirteen."

"Wow, they just get younger and younger, don't they?" The policeman asked his partner, who agreed emphatically.

"But, officer," Lindsay shakily tried to explain, "I didn't do anything wrong. I wasn't going to drink the beer. I just had to buy it for a dare. I would never have actually drunk it."

"It doesn't matter. You are a minor, and even attempting to purchase alcohol has a penalty of a huge fine and all kinds of other legal problems," the officer said, wanting to scare her. "This is very serious. I'm going to need to get some information from you."

The policeman asked some questions that

Lindsay answered, but she was having a difficult time focusing on his words. Her thoughts were swimming, and she began to panic. Then she noticed that her friends were being loaded into the back of a squad car by the other policeman.

"Where are you taking my friends?" Lindsay wanted to know, wiping at the streaming tears on her cheeks. She realized that she was alone in her trouble. Even Kelly, who had drunk a whole can of beer, had waited outside with the others while Lindsay carried out her dare alone, so she had escaped close scrutiny from the police.

"They are being taken home. The officer will speak to their parents, but they aren't in any trouble—other than whatever their parents deem appropriate for them being out so late, of course. You, on the other hand, will be accompanying me to the station."

Lindsay began to weep, her shoulders shaking under the enormity of the situation. How could she have gotten herself into this mess? What was she thinking? Suddenly the words hit her: "Sin creeps in silently, slowly. . . ."

The officer led her to the black-and-white

squad car and helped her into the backseat. Mercifully he chose not to use handcuffs, although he could have, he told her. She endured the short ride to the police station in silence, sure that her parents would be there waiting for her when she arrived. Pulling into the parking lot, however, Lindsay didn't see their car. On one hand, she was relieved because the thought of facing them was just too much for her to bear. But on the other hand, she felt so alone and vulnerable walking into the police station led by one policeman and followed by another. She was under arrest, and no amount of wishing or begging was going to make this go away.

Lindsay was led to a seat in a small room where a policewoman was sitting at a desk, ready to take down her information. "Lindsay, I'm not going to question you about the crime until your parents are here, but I do need to get some information from you and process you before they will be allowed in."

She began to ask Lindsay questions like

her name, her parents' names, her address, where she went to school, how old she was, and how many siblings she had.

The questions continued for a long time with no thought or concern for the tears falling down her face. It wouldn't have mattered, anyway; there was no way she could have controlled her tears. She answered the questions as best she could, but mostly her thoughts were consumed with dread over the moment when her parents would arrive. She wanted them to be there to comfort her, but she couldn't stand the thought of seeing their disappointment and anger.

She was taken back to her seat and told that Officer Marshall was talking with her parents and would bring them in to see her in a moment. Lindsay's heart sank at the very thought of facing them. She could never have imagined how painful regret would be. It was like a knife driving through her heart. What she wouldn't give to go back and do the whole thing all over again. She would have made a far different choice. But it was too late.

She heard a door open and then slam shut, the lock sliding into place. Lindsay listened with dread to the sound of hollow footsteps on the tile floor until they stopped at the doorway to her holding room. She looked up and, at that moment, felt the agony that was visible on her mother's swollen, tear-streaked face. She looked as though a loved one had died—in some ways, one had. Her dad was stone-faced, emotionless, in shock. He clearly didn't know how to react or what to do.

"Should we have a lawyer here?" he asked Officer Marshall.

The officer informed her parents that no questioning had taken place yet, so they were free to call an attorney if they wished. But, the officer also promised, if they began the questioning process without the attorney, they could stop at any time should they decide to call one. He assured them that he just wanted to sort out the details and then they could be on their way.

"Well, let's just get to the bottom of this thing, then," Lindsay's dad said quietly, resigned to the fact that this was not going to be enjoyable for any of them.

"Lindsay, I'm going to turn on this tape recorder now. It just saves me from having to write a lot of notes." When Lindsay nodded, the officer continued. "Let's just make this a bit easier on all of us. Rather than me peppering you with all sorts of questions, why don't you just tell us what happened?"

Lindsay, grateful to be able to tell her side of the story, started at the very beginning, with the first sleepover and the first time they played Truth or Dare. When she finished her story, her mom had finally stopped crying and was able to speak. "Lindsay, what you've done is very wrong. Aside from the many, many ways that you broke our rules and the rules at the Garretts' home, didn't you realize that attempting to buy alcohol was illegal?"

"No, Mom, I had no idea. I knew it was illegal to drink it. But I never knew it was illegal to even buy it. I told the shopkeeper that my dad had sent me to the store for it, so I thought he would sell it to me since it wasn't for me."

"So on top of all of the rules *and* laws you broke, you lied and risked your father's reputation. You know how we feel about alcohol. To think that your dad would drink that beer, let alone send *you* to the store to buy it—it's awful."

Her head in her hands, she continued. "Oh, Lindsay, what I wouldn't give to have just listened to you and kept you home from that sleepover."

"So what happens now?" Lindsay's dad asked Officer Marshall.

"Lindsay will be given a court date that I will get for you before you leave. The judge will almost certainly require that she attend an alcohol-awareness class. I would recommend that Lindsay go ahead and do that now, before court. It will show the judge that she is concerned about what has happened and is becoming educated in the dangers and laws about alcohol. It can't hurt her, but it sure could help things. I can give you information about local groups who offer those classes before you leave tonight."

The officer left them to sit alone in the room while he gathered the information that he had offered to them. No one said a word in that small room. In the deafening silence, Lindsay felt as though the walls were closing in on her. All she wanted was for her mom to take her in her arms and hold her, promising that everything would be just fine—but Lindsay knew that she couldn't do that yet. So, she remained very alone in her regret and her fear.

The officer returned, had each of them sign a few papers, and gave them copies of everything they signed, as well as instructions for her court appearance—which was a full ninety days away. Lindsay sighed. The uncertainty of this would be hanging over her head for at least that long.

The Martins were escorted to the door, and they left the station. At the car, Lindsay began to climb into the backseat and realized that she would never be able to get into the backseat of a car without remembering how it felt to be a common criminal on her way to jail. Nothing would ever be the same for Lindsay—or for any of them.

Chapter 10

CONSEQUENCES

The weeks that followed her arrest were even more difficult than Lindsay had imagined they could be. Not only had she been forced to face her parents' disappointment, but she'd also been the subject of whispers and secret conversations everywhere she went. At church, the youth council had a meeting about her and she was asked to step down from her new student-leader position in the youth group. At school, her teachers and guidance counselors no longer saw her as an exemplary student; she had become an example of a bad seed. In an attempt to make an example of her, she had even been suspended for three days.

It seemed unfair that she was the only one who got suspended, but Lindsay didn't wish trouble on her friends—even though they did seem to be avoiding her.

She lived in constant fear and dread of the court date looming in the distance. Would she really have to spend time in jail or a juvenile facility? People told her that there was no way that it could happen for her first offense and for something so minor. But others, including her attorney, told her that her particular judge, rather than letting kids off easy, sometimes liked to make examples of young people as a deterrent for other kids.

She also had to attend the drug and alcohol meetings that Officer Marshall had recommended. Of all her punishments, those meetings were by far the worst. She sat there, twice each week, in the presence of adults who had real problems with drugs and alcohol—true addicts. Some of them were there as part of a probation deal, others were court ordered, and some were there voluntarily. But none of them were there as a thirteen-year-old girl who had tried to buy a beer, having never actually tasted alcohol in her life. She felt so conspicuously out of place, sure that no one understood why she was there at all.

Her parents agreed that it was a good idea for her to attend the meetings because she could see firsthand how poor decisions caused big problems for people. She had to watch a video about people whose children were killed by drunk drivers. She learned about diseases and other horrible things that happened to drug users. It was a dark and very real glimpse at a world that Lindsay had never expected to see.

But far, far worse than any punishment or any meeting that she had to attend, Lindsay suffered under the crushing weight of her parents' disappointment. Every time she looked at them, she saw sadness in their eyes. She longed for the lighthearted days when happiness and trust filled her home. Lindsay knew that her parents blamed themselves, which made it even harder for her. She wished that it could be like when she was a little girl and did something wrong. The punishment was swift and just and then over. She wondered if the consequences of this mistake would ever end.

"Mom…" Lindsay hesitated as she walked into the family room where her mom was sitting and staring at a book whose pages she hadn't turned in over an hour.

"Yes, Lindsay, what is it?" her mom gazed up at her and tried to smile, but she still looked tired and sad.

Lindsay couldn't figure out what to say to get things back to the way they had been before. "Oh, nothing, Mom. Would you like for me to start dinner?"

"That would be nice, Lindsay. There's a box of frozen fried chicken in the freezer. You can just put that in the oven and make some macaroni and cheese. It'll be good to sit down and talk as a family over dinner."

Lindsay's heart sank. By *talk*, she knew that her mother meant Lindsay would have to listen to her parents tell her once again just how disappointed they were and how she would have to work hard to regain their trust.

She wanted to run, to hide, to pretend that everything was the same as it had been before the stupid dare. Instead she trudged into the kitchen to start dinner.

A month had gone by since that fateful night. Lindsay couldn't bear her parents' looks of disappointment any longer. Every time she was with them, she felt her guilt weighing heavily on her. She didn't want to carry it anymore, but she wasn't sure how to get rid of it. Lindsay felt like her parents only thought she was sorry because she had been caught. She just wasn't sure how to get them to see how truly sorry she was for what she did so that they would start believing in her again.

Then, Saturday afternoon during her quiet time, she read Proverbs 28:13: "He who conceals his sins does not prosper, but whoever confesses and renounces them finds mercy."

That's it! Lindsay had told her parents what she'd done, but she'd never confessed the sin behind it. She closed her Bible and stood up with purpose, resolved to finally put this to rest. Finding her mom upstairs folding laundry and her dad cleaning out the garage, Lindsay knew it was time to bring them together for a talk.

"Mom?" Lindsay called up the stairs.

"What, Lindsay?" Her mom called back.

"Can you come down here for a minute? I want to talk to you and Dad."

"I'll be right down."

When Lindsay heard that, she went to the garage door so she could call for her dad only to see that he was already on his way back into the house. "Oh good. I was just coming to get you. I'd like to talk to you and Mom, if you don't mind."

"Nothing has happened, has it?" Mr. Martin asked with a panicked tone.

"No, no, nothing like that. Just have a seat. Mom is on her way down."

When both of her parents were seated on the couch and looking at her with questioning eyes, Lindsay sat down in the chair opposite them but then jumped up again, nervous about how to say what she needed to say.

"Mom and Dad, I've asked for this opportunity to talk to you for several reasons. Mainly I want to tell you how sorry I am. I know I've said it before, but this is different. I'm not just sorry that I made a bad decision or that I got caught or even that I'm being punished—I deserve that, I know. I'm also just so very sorry because what I did wasn't just *wrong*, it was a *sin*." Lindsay sounded excited at the announcement of her realization.

Her parents looked at each other and then back at her, their faces not quite as stern as they'd been before. "Go on," her mom said.

"When Kelly told me what the dare was and if I didn't do it that I'd be kicked out of the group, I didn't really think about what it would mean to do it even though I knew it was wrong. I didn't think about how I would appear to the girls by willingly going along with something that my heart was telling me not to do."

Mr. Martin leaned forward, hands clasped together. "Why do you think your heart was telling you not to do it?"

"I think. . ." Lindsay swallowed hard, not sure exactly how to put her thoughts into words. "I think it was God telling me it was wrong. I think it was my conscience—the Holy Spirit— trying to show me that what I was about to do was a sin."

"But do you understand why it was a sin?" Mrs. Martin asked, tears sparkling in her eyes.

"I think so. I think it's because by doing it,

I wasn't being a good witness to the girls. I wasn't showing them that being a Christian means choosing to do things that are right, things that are good and holy, and choosing *not* to do things that are wrong—especially when it's illegal."

Lindsay ran out of steam and put her head in her hands and began to cry. A month of regret and fear had finally broken her. She was heartsick over the way she had ignored God's will and hurt her parents but so grateful for forgiveness and unconditional love.

Instantly her mom was at her side and her dad wasn't far behind. They were holding her and rocking her back and forth. Both of them were crying, too.

"Oh, Lindsay, sweetheart," her mom cried. "We have been praying so hard that you would finally come to understand this, that you'd understand we were still hurting. You hadn't asked God for forgiveness yet, and we couldn't force you to do it when you weren't ready."

"You've proven to us that you've learned from your mistake, Lindsay," her dad said, his voice gruff with emotion. "There is a difference between being sorry that you got into trouble and true repentance. We've been praying for you to find your way to true repentance." He paused for a moment. "Speaking of prayer, the one thing that I've missed most is that we haven't been praying together as a family since this happened."

"Yes!" Lindsay wiped at her tears. "I've missed praying with you guys so much! But I just couldn't do it because every time I thought about it, the guilt was so terrible that I couldn't breathe."

The three Martins joined hands. Lindsay felt an electric spark at the touch of her parents' hands. She realized that it had been almost a month since she had let either of them do that.

With a deep breath, her dad began, "Father, we come to You broken and sinful. Not one of us is perfect. We have all sinned and fallen short of Your goodness and grace. We need You now more than ever. Please fill us with Your peace, Your grace, Your wisdom. Thank You, Father, for answering our prayers and leading Lindsay back to You, back to her family. Unite us as a family once again."

"Jesus," Lindsay began to pray, "please, please forgive me for what I did. Help me to find forgiveness from those around me. Please show me how to rebuild the reputation that I have destroyed by my actions. And, Jesus, please help me to face my consequences and get through this time with my head held high. If You can use me in some way to reach other kids through this, please just show me how."

"Heavenly Father, I thank You for my family." Mrs. Martin's voice caught as she began to cry once again. "I thank You for my daughter, who has found her strength in You and, like the little lost lamb, has come back into the fold. Please unite us, and help us get Lindsay through this time. Lord, please let Lindsay know just how much we love her. Show us how to help her and give us wisdom to know what to do."

The Martins all said, "Amen," at the same time, united once again.

Chapter 11

THE FREEDOM OF FORGIVENESS

"Morning, Mom," Lindsay said cheerfully, as she bounced into the kitchen. She looked refreshed and happy, like she'd had a great night's sleep. Mrs. Martin smiled back at her daughter, reflecting the same sense of relief and buoyancy as Lindsay.

"What's gotten into you?" Mrs. Martin teased.

"Oh nothing, really—I'm just relieved. Plus I have some work to do, and I'm anxious to get started on it."

"Work? What kind of work?" Lindsay's mom asked as she passed the milk so Lindsay could pour it over her cereal.

"Well, you and Dad and God aren't the only ones I need to fix things with. But I'm not really sure how to get started."

"You could start by talking with Pastor Steve. Tell him what you told us last night, and I know he'll be able to pray with you and maybe even give you a Bible study that will help you learn how to make better decisions in the future."

"That's a good idea. And I feel like I need to apologize to Sam's, Macy's, and Kelly's parents. They've always been so good to me, and I feel like I've really let them down."

"Maybe you could write each girl's parents a letter," her mom suggested. "I think that they all understand you weren't completely at fault, but taking responsibility for your actions will go a long way toward regaining their trust."

"Actually I think I'd rather talk to them—I want to ask for their forgiveness face-to-face so they can hopefully see that I mean what I say." Lindsay took a few bites of cereal. "Then I need to talk to the girls. I don't know if our friendship can ever be the same; after all, they did tell me that if I didn't do the dare, they wouldn't be my friends anymore. I can't just ignore that and pretend it didn't happen."

"I know you've been friends with them for a very long time, Lindsay," Mrs. Martin said, "but if they're going to put those kinds of conditions on your relationship, are you sure they're the right friends for you?"

Lindsay laid her spoon down on the table. "First I'll explain to them about why what I did was wrong—about how it was a sin and how I've confessed it to God and prayed for forgiveness. But then I'll explain that from now on I can only be friends with them as long as they don't pressure me to do things I know are wrong. If they can't agree to that, I'll have to tell them we can't hang out anymore. It'll hurt, but I know that I need to be strong and do what's right. So I'll do my best."

"Well, Linds, it sounds like you have a really full day ahead of you. I think it's a wonderful thing that you're doing. Do you want me to drive you?"

"No, thank you. I'd really rather take care of all this on my own. I mean, if that's okay. I know I'm grounded, but I promise I won't hang out or socialize."

"Lindsay, your dad and I feel that your punishment here at home has run its course. You've grown beyond what being grounded was teaching you. So, yes, I think it's fine and probably for the best that you go alone. I'll be praying for you the whole time, though." Mrs. Martin reached across the table and hugged her daughter tightly.

Lindsay gave her mom a kiss, grabbed her bag, and left the house with a skip in her step. She was so happy to be back on the right track, and it showed in her every movement and on her face.

First stop: the church.

Lindsay hopped on her bicycle and headed for the church. It took her almost thirty minutes to bike there, but it was a nice ride; the exercise and fresh air did her some good by clearing her mind and helping her prepare for her conversation with Pastor Steve. When she arrived at the church, she paused for a moment to take a drink of water from the water bottle in the holder on her bike. As she was standing there drinking her water, Pastor Steve pulled into the parking lot. He saw Lindsay and walked right up to her.

"Hey, Lindsay. How are you today?"

"I'm fine, Pastor Steve. I was hoping that we could have a chat. Do you have a few minutes?"

"Absolutely. Let me put my stuff down, and I'll meet you in the youth center, okay?" Pastor Steve, wearing his usual blue jeans and polo shirt, took his brown gym bag and lunch bag into the church. When he came back through the parking lot, walking toward the youth center, Pastor Tim was with him.

"Lindsay," Steve began when he opened the door to the youth center, "do you mind if Pastor Tim joins us. . .or is there some reason that you'd like to speak privately?"

"No, actually that's great, because I was going to head into the church to talk with him when we got finished, so this works out great."

"So what's up?" The two pastors waited for her to collect her thoughts and begin.

"You probably know what I'm here for, and I'm sure you know all or most of the details about the events that happened. What I'd like to share goes back just a little bit before that, though." They nodded and remained silent, encouraging her to continue.

"Pastor Tim, about a month ago, before all of this happened, you preached a sermon about avoiding even the appearance of evil. And you explained about how sin creeps in and we aren't even aware of it until it's too late unless we're prepared for it."

"Well, at least I know that someone was listening." The pastor winked at her.

"Yeah, it really stuck with me. Actually, immediately after the sermon, before I left the church, I was able to put it into practice. I happened upon some kids who were messing around with cigarettes, and I realized that if I stayed with them and we were caught, even if I wasn't doing the bad behavior, I would be accused of it or at least of condoning it just by associating with them. Right?"

"Absolutely, Lindsay. That's exactly what I was talking about in my sermon."

"Well, look what happened to me. I guess I don't mean 'happened' to me, because it was my own doing. But it was a real live case of sin creeping in slowly and doing something that I didn't realize was so bad but has cost me a lot."

They both nodded their understanding, so Lindsay continued. "So, I guess what I'm here for is to ask for your forgiveness. I know that I disappointed both of you and deeply affected your trust in me even after you gave me a leadership role. I am just so sorry, and I hope that someday our relationship and trust can be restored."

"Lindsay," Pastor Steve jumped in, "we absolutely forgive you. Thank you for sharing with us. It's awesome to see such real understanding and application from someone your age. I am really proud of you. While I can't restore your leadership role just yet, it's still there and it's yours when the time is right. In the meantime, I wonder if you would be willing to share what you've told us with the youth group. Many young people would benefit from hearing your experiences and would hopefully apply them before they got into trouble. Would you do that?"

"I—I don't know if I'm quite ready to share yet with the whole youth group. I really need to work on straightening things out with my friends first, and I don't know how long that will take. But I might be able to share some of it eventually, even though it'll be really hard—I'll need to pray about it a lot to make sure my heart is really right with God before I do."

"Lindsay, my heart is so full of joy right now." Pastor Tim wiped his eyes. "I was grieved by what transpired, and I have prayed for you and your family nonstop since the beginning of all of this. I can see that my prayers have been answered mightily. You are an inspiration to me, young lady."

The pastors asked if they could pray with Lindsay before she left. During their prayer, Lindsay felt another piece to her puzzle of healing falling into place. She knew that another empty part of her had been filled by their forgiveness. As she rode her bike toward her neighborhood, she let the wind blow in her face—she felt so free.

One by one, Lindsay went to speak with the girls' moms, leaving Macy's mom for last. Kelly's mom was a little standoffish at first. But then she admitted that she admired Lindsay's strength and that she knew she hadn't acted alone. She said that she hoped the girls would be able to have the same old friendship back really soon but that it would be awhile before she would allow Kelly to attend a sleepover. Lindsay understood—she wasn't sure she wanted to go to a sleepover anytime soon, anyway. She didn't stay long—just long enough to make sure she said all she needed to.

At Sam's house, she was received much more warmly by Mrs. Lowell. "Oh, honey, you don't need to apologize to me. You sweet thing, you didn't do anything wrong. You didn't know."

"Mrs. Lowell, with all due respect, I did do many things wrong, and it's important that I own up to them. Whether or not I knew it was illegal, I knew in my heart it was wrong. Regardless of the involvement of the other girls, I want to take responsibility for my part. I feel the need to apologize to you for the bad example I was to Sam and for breaking your trust in me."

"Oh, you sweet thing. Don't give it another thought. Boy, your parents sure did things right with you. I'd like to know their secret."

"Their secret is easy: God is a daily part of our lives. They live the way they want me to live, and they uphold His high standards for me. That's all there is to it. Thanks a lot for your time,

Mrs. Lowell. I have to be going now."

Sam's mom reached over and gave Lindsay a hug. "Say. . .if you can let any of that God stuff rub off you and onto Sam, I'd sure be appreciative."

"I'll do my best, Mrs. Lowell. I promise."

For the last stop on her road to forgiveness, Lindsay pulled into the Monroes' driveway. Macy was sitting on the front porch by herself, looking sad and bored. When she saw Lindsay pull into the driveway, she perked up immediately. "Lindsay!" Macy ran to her and hugged her. "I know I see you in school, but it seems like so long since I've been able to really see you."

"I know, Mace. I miss you, too. It's been a long month. Unfortunately, I'm not here for social reasons today. I promised my parents that I would come and do what I needed to do and then head home. Things are getting a lot better, though. It won't be long until we can get caught up. I promise."

"Okay, Linds. So what are you here for, then?"

"I just need to talk to your mom, if she's

around. You can come, too, if you want."

The girls walked into the cheery kitchen, where Mrs. Monroe was pouring hot coffee into a big mug. The dishwasher was running, and she had a magazine tucked under her arm.

"Mom, Lindsay is here to see you. She wants to talk to you."

"Well, hello there, Lindsay. Why don't you two come out to the back porch with me? I just finished cleaning up the kitchen, and I was about to take my coffee outside. So it's perfect timing."

Macy and Lindsay went outside. Mrs. Monroe sat on the white wicker glider that faced the chairs the girls sat in. "So, what's happening, Lindsay? What can I do for you?"

"Mrs. Monroe, I'll get right to the point, and I won't take up too much time. I am here to apologize to you for the things that I did and the bad influence I was on Macy. I really blew it, and the worst part is that you trusted me and expected me to have higher standards. So I wanted to apologize to you, especially." Lindsay went on to tell her of all the things that she had learned over the past month. By the time they were through talking, all three of them were crying.

"Lindsay, even in the midst of the worst trouble you have ever been in, you still manage to become an example that I want to hold up before Macy's eyes."

"Mrs. Monroe, the thing is, I am just like each of us. I am a human being who makes mistakes. But I am also forgiven by God. He offers that forgiveness to everyone and then calls us to a higher standard. It's perfectly all right to make mistakes, but it's not okay to keep making the same ones or to stay mired in them. Does that make sense?"

"Complete sense. I hope that you continue to grow into the young woman that you're becoming. And, please, don't be a stranger. We'd like to see you around here more. It's been a while."

"Thanks, Mrs. Monroe, I appreciate it so much. I'll be back as soon as my parents start to feel more comfortable with me having more freedom. It'll just take some time."

They hugged and wiped their eyes. Macy walked Lindsay to her bike in the driveway, and Lindsay hopped on and started for home. She felt so free. She had done what she set out to do that day, and it felt great. There was just one more thing to do. . . .

"Hi, girls."

Lindsay was leaning against the big tree in front of the school when Macy, Kelly, and Sam got there the next morning. It was the first time since the last sleepover that Lindsay had joined them in the morning.

"Hi, stranger," Sam said. Macy just smiled.

Kelly stared at her for a minute. "I don't get why you've been hiding from us. I mean, are you angry with us?"

"I'll admit, Kelly, I was angry. But I'm over that. I had to get to the point where I was accepting responsibility for my own actions rather than blaming you guys. I was mad because I felt like I wasn't given the choice to not do the dare. I felt like my choice was to either just do it or lose your friendship. Like I said, I got over being mad because it was my choice, but I guess I felt like our friendship must not have meant as much to you if it was so easy for you to dispose of it when I didn't do what you said."

"Wow, I guess I can see how you would feel that way. We got carried away that night, didn't we?" Kelly asked.

Lindsay chuckled. "Yeah, I think that's safe to say. It's okay, though; I really am glad it happened. It brought my family closer together and closer to God. I now truly understand forgiveness. It's fine with me if you roll your eyes, Kell. It's just part of who I am. Can you accept me for me or not?"

"Of course I can, Lindsay. I'm so sorry that I pressured you and made you feel like you would lose our friendship."

"It's okay. It's not your fault that I did what I did. But if we are going to be friends, I just need to know that I can be myself 100 percent and not have to pretend I'm someone I'm not."

"It's a deal. Lindsay, I'm sorry."

"I'm sorry, too."

The four girls hugged each other for a long time. It felt so good to be back where they belonged—together. The bell rang, signaling the start of the school day, so the four girls walked together, arm in arm, up the stairs to the school. Lindsay watched their reflection in the front doors of the school. What she saw there were the same four girls whose reflections she had seen in that same door on the first day of school— only now they were wiser and stronger. Lindsay smiled at the thought of all they had been through and grinned even wider when she realized how far they had yet to go together. God was good.

My Decision

I, *(include your name here)*, have read the story of Lindsay Martin and have learned from the choices that she made and the consequences that she faced. I want to make choices that lead my life down the path that God has for me. I promise, from this moment on, to think before I act and, in all things, to choose God's will over mine. Specifically, I will honor my parents and avoid disobedience, even when I don't think my behavior is really wrong.

Please pray the following prayer:

Father God, I don't know everything, and I can't possibly have everything under control. Please help me remember the lessons I've learned as I've read this book. Help me to honor my parents and serve You by making right choices and avoiding questionable situations. It is my desire to be a witness to others about Your grace and love. I know I can't do that if my behavior is questionable. So if I get in a tight spot, please help me to find a way out and give me the strength to do what it takes. I know that You have everything under control, so I submit to Your will. Amen.

Congratulations on your decision! Please sign this contract signifying your commitment. Have someone you trust, like a parent or a pastor, witness your choice.

_____

Signed

_____

Witnessed by

If you enjoyed

TRUTH OR DARE

look for more
Interactive Fiction
for Girls

Magna
and
Making Waves

Coming soon to a bookstore near you.